CHOOSE ME

By Nicole Spencer-Skillen

This is a work of fiction. Names, characters, places
and incidents either are the product of the author's
imagination or are used fictitiously. Any resemblance
to actual people, living or dead, events or locales, is
entirely coincidental.

First Edition: November 2020

Edited by Megan Georgia

Cover by Lewis McMullen @for.you.creative

Dedications

To my wife, thank you for always supporting me in everything I do, from listening to me read my book to helping me bring the cover to life; I can't thank you enough for always being there. I love you.

****

Mum, you bought me all the books I wanted when I was growing up, you gave me the freedom to read/write as much as I pleased, leaving me to delve deep into my imagination as a child, even if you did have to check I was still alive sometimes! Thank you for everything.

CHAPTER ONE

It's heart-breaking, the end of a relationship: The final goodbye that signifies the end of an era and the start of a new, unknown beginning. That is where our lives often hang in the balance—the choice between doing what you think is right or what you know is right. The decisions are inevitably our own; therefore, we have to live with the consequences.

Do I believe that it is altogether easy? I very much doubt it, but what's worth it in the end is never easy; That, I truly do believe.

My name is Holly Garland and I am 28 years old. I haven't lived the most exciting life - I guess you could say I have yet to live - but I have loved. I have loved deeply, passionately and purely, with everything I have. Not many 28 years old can say that. Not many can say they had the courage to walk away when it was no longer what they hoped it would be.

I am far from perfect; I will be the first to admit that. I am your average woman in every way. I have a great family and a small circle of friends, an excellent job for my age (it gets me a nice car and a penthouse apartment), but I have always preferred my home comforts. I love to be sat in front of the TV, in my sweats with a big bar of chocolate.

I stand at 5'8" with long, brown hair and dark green eyes. I have always been a bit of a skinny girl; the gym and I have never been the best of friends, but, thankfully, I have a very high metabolism which means I can survive without it for now. I always struggle to find the motivation to work out, often opting for the easier option of ordering a takeaway and pretending that I will take out a gym membership the next day. There are too many people that are obsessed with their fitness these days. In all honesty, I admire the resilience and the motivation they possess to be such a way, but I was never made for a life of dieting, *'you only live once'* being the cliché line. Why spend it eating salads?

I love my job and not a lot of people can say that. I was always told that if you find a job you love, you will never have to work a day in your life. This, I have found, is true. I spent a lot of time preparing for my role as a lawyer - 6 years of hard work and course after course - but I wouldn't change it for the world. At the tender age of 16, I had decided that I wanted to follow in my father's footsteps and become a lawyer. From then on, it's all I have focused on and now, as I write this, I have been fully qualified for four years.

I toyed with a few alternative job prospects when I was younger, a postwoman being the highlight of them all. I have the utmost respect for how quickly they can deliver letters after struggling my way through a 6-month, temporary role alongside my studies. It certainly wasn't the job for me. I started at a law firm based in London called West & Barnes when I was 22 to complete my 2-year training contract.

After working there for two years, I was debating what to do next. I had received offers from several different law firms but, when West & Barnes offered me a full-time role as a criminal lawyer, I couldn't turn it down. I decided there and then that I would do everything within my power to make something of myself.

The idea of studying law and becoming a lawyer had always appealed to me. They seemed to live such a high life, full of compelling cases and conspiracies. When I got to know a few of the law firm's lawyers, I quickly realised how much hard work and how many long hours it took before the job gets to be anything like what we all see on the TV.

Luckily, I had found the determination to be the best, ultimately growing to love my job in those first two years. The people I met and the bonds I made were unbreakable and, after much debate, I knew that continuing my career as a criminal lawyer with West & Barnes was the best thing for me to do.

The prospects within the company were just too good to turn down. It has taken me four short years to get to where I am today. I worked my way into The Lawyer Hot 100 two years in a row (something I am unbelievably proud of), and my case wins were starting to become recognised country-wide.

I live and work in London, a city like no other, in my eyes. Nobody has truly experienced the hustle and bustle of London unless you have lived there. It's a truly magical place to live. I moved around a lot in my younger life, but I moved to London ten years ago at the age of eighteen, to a place called Bloomsbury. It's known for its high culture, boasting the likes of the British Museum and Beautiful Garden Squares; It's got a distinct village-feel, strange for a place that is well in the midst of central London. I originally moved there for educational reasons, reasons that eventually led me to *her*.

Where do I begin? Everyone remembers their first love; It's magical and mesmerizing, and everything you hoped it would be, but that doesn't always last. That is the agonising truth, the fact that your first love is very rarely your last love. Maybe a part of you will always be with that person because they once held the very best of you, your innocence and belief that love lasts forever. I was not one of the rare few, but I do not regret a single second of my time with her.

Eight years, we had together. We formed so many memories – granted, some were good and others bad, but they were memories all the same. In the beginning, I would've given anything to make her happy; I had fallen for her completely. It only took a year for us to move in together. I genuinely thought that I had found the girl I wanted to spend the rest of my life with.

Through no fault of hers or my own, it just wasn't meant to be, and I soon realised I was holding on to something I had given up fighting for long ago. When you finally realise it's time to let go, every emotion possible enters your body. I don't like to think that I gave up, but she will always see things differently to me and, for that, I am truly sorry. I like to think I gave it everything I had.

I fought for the years of memories, for the future plans made and for us, but mainly for her.

I fought so that I wouldn't have to break her heart so that I wouldn't have to see the tears roll down her face, the tears I had spent so many years wiping away. The person she relied on and trusted to always love her and always be there was now the reason those tears fell.

There is one regret I will always have: I couldn't make myself stay. I couldn't save her that heartbreak. She didn't deserve that; nobody does.

Although your first love always seems so significant, this story is not about my first love. It is about the privilege I had of meeting my true love, my soul mate.

CHAPTER TWO

It was like any other ordinary day at work. I arrived at the office at 8 am. By half past, I had answered the phone three times and replied to six emails. The standard for a Friday morning. I had my first meeting of the day at 9 am, and I was scheduled pretty much back to back for the whole day.

It was October, which meant that the streets felt significantly busier and more people would pop in on the off chance they could get an appointment. I had been the only lawyer in the West & Hayes firm to be featured in the Top 100 in the last ten years. This meant that more and more people had started to request my name in the hope I would take on their cases.

My average caseload was around 25 at any one time, but that quickly lowered to 15 as the company wanted me to take on more complex cases. These problematic cases required a lot more of my time, making it even more difficult for people to acquire my services.

The streets were busy due to the commencement of Christmas shopping. A mass of people, short, tall, large, thin, every type of person you could imagine, were out in droves. Everyone was wrapped up in their latest winter fashion accessories, bracing the coldest weather for over a decade so that they could get the latest high street bargains. If there was one thing people on Regents Street in London knew how to do, it was shop.

I was much more of a sale shopper, myself, and sale days were always my favourite. When you work on one of London's busiest shopping streets, it can be hard to resist.

There was always a new face in the office, but I rarely got the chance to get to know them before the next one came along. We had interns, trainee lawyers and legal assistants come and go on a regular basis.

There was, however, one face that caught my eye on that particular day. I later found out she had worked for us for almost two years but on a different floor, which explained why I hadn't seen her before. Her name was Brooke Jacobs, and she had recently transferred to become a legal assistant on the criminal law floor. We encountered one another late that afternoon and the conversation from that day was crystal clear in my mind.

There she was, standing in the doorway of my office, looking hesitant and sheepish.

"Hi, what can I do for you?"

"Hi, my name's Brooke. I'm the new legal assistant. Nice to meet you."

She strode confidently over to my desk and extended her hand.

"Hi, Brooke. I'm Holly Garland. Nice to meet you too."

"I know exactly who you are; I saw you in the paper the other day. Amazing work you did with the Johnson case and the Barello case before that. I'm a big fan of your work."

So, she was an avid reader. I liked people that did their homework.

"I appreciate that, thank you. Are those documents for me?"

Brooke clutched a folder in her arms, which I assumed was the reason she was stood in my doorway.

"Oh, yes, sorry, I should get to the point. Mr West said you would be happy to take on this case. He told me to bring it over to you."

She promptly laid the folder down on my desk.

"Not a problem. I'm just finishing up preparation for court tomorrow, and then I will take a look at it."

I glanced at the clock. It was almost 4 pm; many paralegals would typically be packing up their desk and heading home, providing there were no pressing matters.

"What time are you done today, Brooke?"

She looked surprised at my question.

"I was hoping to be done for 5 pm, I have a date with some girlfriends of mine, but I can stay if you need me?"

I remembered the freedom of my younger years before I was officially qualified. Now, freedom to leave on time was a rarity.

"Only 1 hour to go then, lucky you. It's times like these where I regret being a criminal lawyer; 12-hour days are a prerequisite, it seems. Do you have any tasks for the last hour? I could always use some help with this ridiculous pile of paperwork."

For some reason, I felt the urge to talk to her. I was making conversation that I wouldn't usually make with anyone else at work. It wasn't my job to file the paperwork, that's what we had legal assistants for, but I was always very particular about who helped with my cases. I had been known for being quite blunt, a straight talker who got the job done. I didn't see the point in needless conversations if they weren't going to help me win a case.

"I can imagine the hours are gruelling sometimes; I am yet to experience that. I like to go home at the end of the day and not worry about this place. I know that's probably not what you want to hear. It doesn't really make me the ideal paralegal, does it? Maybe I should be quiet now."

She spoke quickly, her nervousness evident.

I couldn't help but laugh at her. I don't think she realised that she was funny, the type of humour that was natural, not forced. She wasn't trying in the slightest to be funny; the way she spoke and her facial expressions were effortlessly amusing.

"I think you could think differently one day. You have already taken the leap to be a paralegal, which means the hours will get longer, case dependant. I know a few people that thought the same as you, then as soon as they got their teeth stuck into an interesting case, they forgot time existed."

"Who knows, I feel like I'm too young at the moment to believe my career is my main focus. I'm only 24; I live for holidays with my girlfriends and impromptu nights out."

Brooke loitered by the door.

"I was 22 when I started with this firm, but I was always a bit mature for my age though."

"And look at everything you've achieved! You're inspiring so many young, aspiring lawyers. I'm sure that if or when the day comes that I want to take that leap, I will be looking at you for guidance. And, if I am completely honest with you, I did think you were about 35, but I know that you've been here six years, according to your online profile, so that makes you... 28?"

I pretended to look offended.

"Oh, you did? It worries me slightly that everyone thinks I am at least six years older than I am. Do I really have that many wrinkles?"

I looked in the mirror on my desk.

"No, it's not that! You are just ridiculously mature for your age. I mean, look how settled you are. You won't catch me living with a long-term partner or being one of the most prolific lawyers of the decade at 28. I will probably still be at home with my Dad."

I was curious to know how she even knew I had a long-term partner or what my lifestyle was like at all.

"How do you know I don't go out on a weekend and party until the sun comes up? I am curious as to how you seem to know so much about me. I don't think my Law profile says I live with my partner."

I think that if I were playing poker, I would have lost, hands down. My poker face is terrible.

"Just an observation; feel free to correct me if I'm wrong. And people talk in this firm, so I got the low down from Paula as soon as I arrived on the floor."

She was confident. I had to give her that, and she wasn't intimidated, not scared in the slightest to challenge me. I liked that, but she was young, not in age but in mind. My job had forced me to mature quickly and, considering most people thought I was 35 years old, I figured I might as well act that way.

"You could be right, to be honest—enough about me. I'll be having words with Paula when I see her; I dread to think what else she's been saying. Why don't you start by filing those documents for me to pass some time? I'll ask you some questions while working, seeing as though you know more about me than I know about you. I don't like being at a disadvantage."

I had very little to finish, which excited me because the prospect of having a weekend off was one I relished. I soon remembered the reason Brooke had come to me in the first place, but I put that case to the back of my mind. I would read it on the way home and hopefully, whatever it was could wait until Monday.

Filing paperwork often became a dull and mundane task to partake in. If it wasn't emails, research, or phone calls that needed to be made, there was always paperwork. Unusually, I found myself distracted and something beyond my control kept me talking to her.

"Okay, what kind of questions?"

She looked puzzled at my request to question her, my lawyer instincts taking over. I had a feeling that if Paula had given her the low down, she would know that I didn't just make conversation with people unnecessarily. The most extended discussions I had in the workplace were with clients.

I preferred it that way. I always thought it better not to mix business and pleasure, so I didn't go out of my way to make friends with people at work. Maybe that's how I'd gotten where I was so quickly. I was undoubtedly driven and all about my career. My first question could have been better considering I was an esteemed lawyer but, equally, I didn't want her to feel like I was interrogating her.

"What's your favourite colour?"

Her response was immediate.

"Purple, you?"

"Emerald green. I don't own anything that colour though, so God knows why.

It was true; I didn't own anything emerald green. Although, I did have two predominantly green paintings hung on my wall at home. She was quick to follow with the next question.

"What about your favourite film?"

"That's a tough one. I would have to say Avatar. Some people think it's too long, but I love it. I find it fascinating that James Cameron spent 15 years and millions of dollars making it. I don't think there's another film like it."

Brooke, who was now facing the filing cabinet, turned back in surprise.

"Are you joking? Avatar is one of my favourite films too! It is so underrated, weirdly none of my friends like it, but I am in awe every time I watch it."

"I agree with you completely. Okay, I'll ask you another. What's your favourite food?"

The most important question of all.

"Sweet or savoury?"

"Both."

She paused. She was contemplating her response.

"Okay, savoury would definitely be anything Chinese, without a doubt. Apple pie or just a good old-fashioned chocolate cake for sweet."

"I 100% agree with both Chinese and chocolate cake. You read my mind."

The conversation continued like that for another 30 minutes. We asked the most random questions and found that, amazingly, most of our answers were exactly the same. We liked the same foods, the same films, the same music - she even liked to do the same things outside of work.

Every question we asked brought us a little bit closer to the realisation that we had almost everything in common.

Much to my disappointment, I had to cut the conversation short, my phone had been endlessly ringing off the hook, and I couldn't avoid it any longer.

It was 8 pm by the time I got home. It turned out the case Mr West had handed me earlier in the day required some urgent attention.

Danielle had my dinner prepared as I walked through the door, as she always did. She would very rarely finish work later than 5 pm, so she always prepared the food. Unless it were

Saturday night, that, without fail, would always be a takeaway night.

She was good to me; I had to give her that. We had been together for eight years, she worshipped the ground I walked on, and I knew that I would never find someone that would love me the way she did. I was her whole life, the sad realisation being that she was not mine. I had known it for a while leading up to that point, but I continued regardless, just hoping that, maybe, I would one day feel the same again.

Danielle Layton, where do I begin? She was a kind-hearted girl, the very best. I met her through a mutual friend many years ago and we instantly hit it off. It was powerful at first, but I think it always is with your first love. Although we didn't have a considerable amount in common, we loved each other deeply. We built a life together, and I knew I loved her. I also knew that the last thing I wanted to do was break her heart, but as the days went on, I grew more disinterested in our relationship. I looked for distractions, ways I could forget that not everything was as it seemed at home. Sadly, I think that was becoming more apparent to her with every passing day.

I gave her a quick kiss, as I so often did when I arrived home, and the usual daily chat started up.

"How was work, babe?"

"It was really good, long but really good. I closed a case today, prepared for another one on Monday, and Mr West dropped an interesting one on me last minute, so that's going to take a lot of time up this weekend. He also set another challenge for the Christmas bonus, which I have every intention of getting."

Mr West was a well-respected lawyer who had practised for over 30 years. He now owned a chain of firms and very rarely fought a case himself. His first name was Martin, but he liked to be called Mr West. Much like myself, he was career-focused and didn't engage in many conversations that didn't involve the law.

Mr West had recently set each lawyer in his firm a challenge of completing 10 cases by the end of the month. The possibility of achieving that all depended on the complexity of the cases you were looking at; some could be quick wins, and others could stretch out for months at a time. Law was a complex study and ever-changing, so it was hard to predict how long a case would take.

Whoever managed the 10 cases would receive a £5000 bonus on their next wage.

Mr West always did a similar challenge around Christmas time. I had got to know him more personally over recent months, and I believed he was a good man. The prize was one that I wanted, without a doubt.

I would often count on my Christmas bonus to buy all my presents, as well as treat myself to some more suitable work clothing. I had my eye on a new winter coat from All Saints. The price tag was a typical £280; I was hopeful that it would go into the next sale.

Being a lawyer meant that I had to look the part. The clothes I wore to work had to scream 'professional' and 'presentable'. This requirement meant that a large sum of my wages would go on expensive, new suits. The typical suits picked up on the high street never seemed to be fitting enough, so I would also have to have them tailored, which increased the price tag even further.

"That's great, babe; sounds like another busy day. I'm sure you will win the challenge, you always do. I thought we could watch a film after dinner?"

Danielle was always interested in my day. It didn't matter where I'd been or what I'd done. I'm not sure she even understood half the things I talked about. To be honest, I got pretty bored of hearing myself talk about them.

"I have so much work to do tonight, I need to focus on this new case whilst it's still fresh in my mind. Can we watch one tomorrow night?"

I saw the disappointment in her face and instantly felt terrible because I knew she was trying. Lately, there had been nothing but arguments and it was draining for both of us. The only thing I wanted to do when I got home was eat and put my feet up, not argue for hours about something ridiculous and unnecessary. I simply didn't have it in me, so work was an outlet for me.

"Yes, that's fine. I can watch one in bed. I will leave you to it after dinner; I'm up early anyway."

For some reason, I found myself thinking about Brooke that night. I wondered how I hadn't seen her before. The building was a considerable size, but whether you were on a different floor or not, most people would bump into each other at some stage. Before I fell asleep with my laptop in hand, one of my last thoughts was, *'I could see us being really good friends'*.

The weekend was over in no time as they always were. The majority had been spent studying my latest case. It was an extremely high-profile client and the news coverage had been extensive. A man was accused of murdering his wife but, from what I could gather, he proclaimed his innocence and there didn't seem to be enough damning evidence to say otherwise. This was the sort of case I lived for. Proving someone's innocence with the odds stacked up against me was a challenge I accepted without hesitation.

It was a Monday morning, a day most would dread. I had been up working most of the night so that I was over-prepared for the day ahead, exactly how I liked to be. Paula collared me ten minutes into a phone discussion with a client, a client that thought they knew better than the lawyer they had paid a considerable amount of money to hire. She saved the day.

"Mr West has just called a meeting, Holly. He needs you in it."

Paula was a criminal paralegal. She had worked for West & Hayes for over 15 years and was undoubtedly one of the best. We had worked on many cases together and she had been the first to help me settle in when I first started at the firm. She was one of the very few people I had developed a close bond with. Paula's value to the firm (and to me) was absolutely untouchable. I wrapped up the conversation with my client, excusing myself as quickly as I could.

When I placed the phone back onto the receiver, I looked up to see Paula stood over by the door, with a massive grin on her face: I knew that mischievous grin.

"There is no meeting, is there?"

"Of course not. I'm sending Jake to Starbucks for some breakfast. What do you want? Also, what are we doing for Halloween next weekend? Work's night out? Lastly, Brooke rang, said something about being assigned to help you with your latest case, and do you want her earlier than eight tomorrow? She mentioned that she would struggle with the train services being delayed."

After I had finished laughing, I couldn't remember a word of what she'd said. If there was one thing Paula was good at, it was talking. I heard Starbucks, and that always sounded like a fantastic idea.

"Paula, you should try breathing. Yes, to Starbucks. Not sure about the Halloween situation; into town after work could be a definite possibility. Come to think of it; I need a good night out."

I paused for a second, trying to remember anything else.

"Did you say something about Brooke Jacobs?"

"Yes, she's been assigned to your case but can't start earlier than eight tomorrow due to train delays. Will that not affect you as well?"

"Okay, no problem, no, I'll figure it out."

I often caught the underground to work as it was so much easier than paying a fortune to park in the centre of London. My car was sat at home, gathering dust, only used when I ventured back home to Newquay.

"I don't know if you want to ring Brooke and let her know. Her numbers over there, I can do it if you want."

There was no hesitation in my response.

"No, it's okay, Paula, I'll get around to it. You can carry on. I know you've got a lot to do."

"Okay, I'll catch up with you later. Have a think about Halloween and let me know."

With that being said, she wandered back out of the office. Paula was certainly a firecracker: She had the brightest red hair imaginable, a very slim figure and stood around 5'3", although she never stood smaller than 5'6" because she constantly wore high heels. It was her trademark.

Paula was in her 40s but would never tell anyone her actual age. If I had to take a guess, I would say 46. She had worked in the industry for a long time and had built a strong relationship with a lot of lawyers and prosecutors in London. She was incredibly stylish for her age; I wouldn't mind being in her shoes at 46.

It got to 7 pm on Monday by the time I called it a day, ready to put my feet up. The day had been a long one - as all Mondays usually were - and all I could think about was my day off on Wednesday. I had booked a day off specifically to do some Christmas shopping. I usually took one day in October and then another in November. Taking a day off was the only way

I could get anything done as I couldn't rely on finishing work at 5 pm.

As much as I loved my job, it was stressful, so the days I actually got to switch off and do my own thing were something to look forward too. As I went to lock my office door behind me, I remembered the one thing I forgot to do.

Ring Brooke.

I quickly grabbed the piece of paper off the side, displaying the number, and headed for the door. If I were going to be working on cases with her in the future, I would need her contact details anyway.

Once I reached the underground, I pulled my phone from my coat as I waited for the next train. It didn't take long before I had composed a quick message, typed in the number from the piece of paper and hit send.

Within a minute, I had a reply that read:

Thank you for getting back to me. I didn't want it to be an issue, appreciate it x

I told myself I shouldn't reply. There wasn't anything to reply too, after all. Nonetheless, I found my fingers typing away rapidly.

Wow, could you of replied any quicker haha x

When I hit the send button, I realised how lame it sounded. Who even says something like that? No way will she reply. I'm just making myself look like a complete fool, and that wasn't something I was used to doing. That was until a reply came back 30 seconds later.

This continued for the whole train journey home, through two changes and the five-minute stroll up to my apartment. It was ridiculous. I couldn't work out if the conversation flirtatious; after all, I didn't want to give off the wrong impression, but it wasn't even like that. I barely knew her, but I could sense just how funny, unique and interesting she was even through a text message—something about her overall demeanour made me want to keep talking.

Obviously, I had a girlfriend. That played on the back of my mind, but Brooke knew that too. I would never want to do anything to upset Danielle. I liked to think of myself as trustworthy and loyal, so knowing the type of person I was, I wasn't doing anything wrong. What was the harm in enjoying a conversation with another girl?

In the back of my mind, small alarm bells had already triggered, but I refused to acknowledge them. My conscience was already jumping to conclusions. I quickly put the unnecessary thoughts to the back of my mind before entering my apartment, finally home, ready to endure the same routine all over again.

CHAPTER THREE

"What do you mean, you're not coming out? We agreed on Friday night, and half of the people are only going out because they like to see you get drunk."

It was 9 am on a wet Thursday morning and I had already heard the same speech from Paula at least three times. My reply had never changed and yet she persisted anyway.

"Paula, listen to me. You are hurting my brain. I forgot I had a family thing. It's Danielle's family, and she told them I would be going. Trust me; I would much rather get out of it. I can't think of anything worse, but that's beside the point. Unless I can come after; leave it with me."

There was a long pause; Paula raised her eyebrows at me, her trademark expression. I wasn't even sure it was normal to do that with your face, but it essentially meant *'you know you want too'*.

"I like the sound of that. Whatever family thing it is, it will not be as interesting as a night out with us, so please make it happen. I need someone to look more stupid than me, considering that I am going as a dead pirate. It doesn't exactly shout out sexy, does it?"

I burst out laughing, wondering just who had convinced her to go as a dead pirate, especially when (in her eyes) she had such a fabulous reputation as a costume expert to uphold.

"Really? A dead pirate? I think you will look quite fetching if I'm honest."

My poker face let me down again, dreadfully.

"Piss off, you. It was all they had left. I should have been more prepared, but maybe, if you didn't run me into the ground at work, I would have more time to prepare for things like this."

I rolled my eyes: I did love our banter; it was the best thing about work.

"What can I say? I am a terrible person and you should tell Mr West, immediately, that you can't work with me anymore."

She threw a pen across the room before exiting with a quick farewell message.

"Sort it out, Garland."

The rest of the day played out as expected. I spent an hour updating some clients on their ongoing cases and chasing any paperwork that I was missing. The time I had left was spent on the Bickmore case.

Brooke had arrived at 7:40 am, earlier than expected, and had been busy researching the long list I had given her the night before. She checked back every hour or two with a progress report and I would watch her bouncing her way across the floor, the spring in her step making her look an inch or two taller than her usual 5'4".

If I could describe her in one way, it would be naturally beautiful. She didn't need make-up, and she didn't need her long, blonde hair to be perfectly straight or perfectly curled. She was a rarity.

I felt someone behind me as I stood, watching the world go by through the window of my 4th-floor office.

"Hey, I think I have something here."

I spun around to see Brooke making her way over to my desk. She placed a piece of paper in front of me.

"Hey, Brooke. What have you got for me?"

I studied the piece of paper; it didn't take long to connect the dots. Brooke had produced evidence that undermined the alibi for the gentleman who was suspected of killing Mrs Bickmore.

I looked up with the biggest smile I could muster.

"Amazing work! Where did you find this?"

I could tell that she was pleased with herself.

"Well, I was researching everything to do with Mr Bickmore and I kept reaching a dead end, but the other suspect's name kept popping up. I thought it would be even better if I could build a case to prove someone else had potentially committed the crime. That way, we prove Mr Bickmore's innocence and catch the real murderer at the same time. The other suspect, Mr Whisham, had an alibi the night of the murder. He said he went for a jog and then stopped at his friend's house on his way back home."

She paused for a second to inhale before she continued to divulge her findings, her excitement sending the information out in a flurry.

"His friend vouched for him but, when I dug a little deeper, the timings are all wrong. I looked at the street cameras outside a nearby coffee shop, and they show Mr Whisham leaving that apartment at 8 pm when the alibi said roughly 9 pm. The murder was committed between 8 pm and 9 pm because Mr Bickmore came home to find his wife in a pool of blood at 9:15 pm. So, that tells me Mr Whisham could have definitely jogged the ten minutes to the Bickmore household, committed the crime and left. What I don't understand is why the police didn't look a little bit further into this."

I was impressed.

"I think that what you've found here could really open the case up. Stay on track with that. We need to gather a bit more evidence, maybe any more cameras that caught him along the way. Someone who could describe seeing a man matching Mr Whisham's description around the house at that time. I can present it to the detectives on the case and see what they think. The good news is I think we might be able to leave on time tonight after that discovery."

I handed the pieces of paper back to a beaming Brooke.

"Okay, I'll get on it straight away. I like the sound of that. I have plans tonight, so I'd love to. I forgot to ask the other day, are you coming out tomorrow night for Halloween?"

If I had a pound for every time someone had asked me that same question in the past week, I would've been a lot better off. I knew everyone was only curious, and it was a compliment that so many people wanted me to go. I explained to her the reason why I couldn't come but that I was going to try and come through afterwards.

"I have no idea what to dress up as though. I think I have left it a bit late."

Brooke looked at me as if to say, don't give me that excuse.

"You're a lawyer, so you must have a million white shirts. Grab an old one, cut it up, put some blood on it and draw a few cuts on your face, and you are good to go. You can just go as a dead you."

The idea wasn't terrible.

"That would be the easiest option, and I do have all those things. What are you going as?"

I was intrigued.

"Well, I am 100% not going as anything dead. I can't be seen out on the square like that, so I'm going as a cat. Typical, really, but a few of the other girls are doing the same thing. No blood, maybe a few whiskers, definitely a tail and some leather trousers. All black, of course. My favourite colour."

She didn't strike me as the type to cover herself in blood.

"Wow, okay, so nothing dead, no blood, got it. Hang on; black is your favourite colour? I thought it was purple?"

"Purple is my favourite colour, yes, but I don't wear purple, just like you don't wear green. Black is black; it makes everybody look better. It's a fact."

The fact I remembered her favourite colour surprised her for a second. Brooke was unbelievably easy to talk to and we laughed throughout our whole conversation.

"Oh, well, maybe I should wear more black. What are you doing tonight? Anything interesting?"

It seemed as though I was just making general conversation, but I wanted to know more about her, what she did, where she hung out. I was intrigued to learn as much as she would allow me to.

"I've got to go to some charity event for my boyfriend's rugby club, but I really do not want to go. All his friends and family are going, though, so I can't exactly get out of it."

I was intrigued by her reluctancy. I could tell from her face, the way she looked down when she spoke about it, that it was the last thing she wanted to do. I wondered if there was trouble in her relationship. It wasn't my place to ask - I hardly knew the girl - but I wanted to. I felt obliged to ask the question.

"Why? If you don't mind me asking."

She paused for a second, maybe questioning how much information she should divulge to someone she barely knew.

"I'd just rather be at home. It's awkward sometimes with him. I won't bore you with it; I would just rather not go."

I could instantly tell that she felt uncomfortable talking about it, so I didn't pry.

"Okay, well, I have a plan. I will call him and tell him you are stuck in the elevator at work and can't get out. It might be a while before maintenance gets here to fix it. Also, that you are sorry and saddened not to be making it to the biggest event of your social year."

When anything turned remotely uncomfortable or serious, I always tried to make a joke out of it; it was something that worked in my favour a lot of the time. Sometimes, it could get me into a spot of trouble. That particular time, thankfully, it made her laugh.

"That would be amazing! You are quite funny when you want to be; I'll give you that."

She smiled shyly.

"I do try. On that note, I have a call in 5 minutes, so I will leave you to crack on."

Before she turned to walk away, she caught my attention once more.

"So, maybe I will see a dead you on Friday then?"

I laughed at the prospect.

"Possibly. Maybe I will see a cat that looks just like you, who knows? Anything is possible."

I already had the speech planned in my head before I got home as to why I needed to leave the family gathering early that coming Friday. I knew it would cause friction between Danielle and me, but I only wanted to split the evening; it's not like I wasn't going at all.

I felt terrible: It had gotten to the point where I would rather do anything or be anywhere than at home. As bad as it may sound, I had exhausted all options in trying to make my relationship better. I thought going on holiday might have fixed something between us, but it didn't. I even thought that redecorating would give us something to do together, but that didn't help either. I even tried to spice things up in the bedroom, but the interest just wasn't there anymore. It had become a monotonous relationship, and I was all out of ideas. Although people might ask why we stayed together, it wasn't such an easy explanation to give.

When you have so much history with someone, it's difficult to see a life without that person. That's why I chose to stay and try to make it work time and time again, not necessarily because I believed it could be what it once was, but for the many happy years we'd had. I owed it to the woman I fell in love with.

"Hi, Dan, you okay?"

"Hi, babe, I'm okay. I have had the longest day at work. I just want to get in bed."

I could see the exhaustion on her face. She had recently been promoted to Team Leader, meaning extra pay, but ultimately more hours and I could see it was taking its toll on her.

"Another long one. Can't handle it, can you."

I gave her a wink and a kiss on the cheek before making my way into the living room. There was nothing better than getting home after a long day, kicking your shoes off and sprawling out on the sofa.

"Cheeky, I can handle it. Just an early start this morning, you know I like my sleep."

"I know you do. Okay, so I have a problem with Friday. Hear me out first."

She popped her head around the door from the kitchen with an unmistakable look of annoyance across her face.

"What do you mean, you have a problem? Don't tell me you don't want to go. This has been planned for weeks, Holly."

"Hold on; I said hear me out. So, Paula mentioned the night out this Friday for Halloween. I'd forgotten all about it, but everyone assumes I am going. I won't live it down if I don't go, so I was just wondering if I could maybe split the evening? I will come to the meal with your family and then go out afterwards."

I could see that it wasn't going to go down well, although I suppose I wasn't surprised.

"You are unbelievable! Honestly, how many times a year do we do something with my family? I can probably count on one hand, and you can't be bothered to stick it out for the full night because you'd rather go out with your friends from work? I have never known anyone as selfish in all my life, Holly. Just do whatever you want. Don't come at all; I'm past caring now. I have had a long day and I'm going to bed."

With that, she was gone. I didn't even have time to try and explain myself, but a part of me felt relieved that I didn't have to spend the night arguing over something I was going to do anyway. I know that sounds awful. Maybe I was a horrible person, perhaps she was right and I was selfish.

I thought about what I wanted and that always came first. I started to question why I turned out that way; it hadn't always been like that. Over the years, I had been worn down, moulded into a person who only cared about themselves and what they wanted.

I was ashamed to admit that.

Danielle didn't speak to me at all the following day, despite my apologies for upsetting her. It didn't change the way she felt or the fact that I had already made my decision. I didn't think it had to be such a big deal: The meal would be done around 9 pm and that's when I would head into the square to meet everyone else. I knew it wasn't all down to the fact I was leaving early; it was the same issue she had never been able to shake.

She hated that I had a life without her. She never went out, despite me constantly telling her to go and enjoy herself. I gave her money; I even offered to buy her new outfits. I wanted her to go out and enjoy herself, but she turned me down so many times, telling me she would rather stay in with me and watch a movie. We could do that any night of the week.

That is what I stressed to her a million times over. We are only young once, and we need to live life whilst we can; go out and meet new people, make new friends, get drunk and wake up the next day remembering absolutely nothing. That's what life was all about, and I chose to do that because I enjoyed it.

I spent the first two years of my relationship staying in, catering to her needs instead of my own, and I was told that's what you do when you get into a serious relationship. I disagree: You don't have to lose yourself to please the person you are with and, if that's the case, then they are the wrong person for you. I would always try and make things better, but I knew when she needed some time, so that's what I gave her.

The end of my workday came quickly. Danielle still wasn't in the best of moods, but she had accepted the fact that I was going out. I just had to get through the meal first, which would be a nightmare in itself.

I had never exactly seen eye to eye with Danielle's family. Her grandparents were lovely (as most are), but her sister was very self-involved, not the type of person I liked to be around. Her mother, Annette, was hard work, to say the least. I don't like liars, and she was a compulsive one. I couldn't believe anything that came out of her mouth. The number of problems she caused for the family through her lying was disgraceful. With that being said, I tried to avoid contact with them as much as possible.

I never said that to Danielle. They were her family, and she loved them regardless; it would only upset her. So, I smiled along at the family events as if I had no opinion on them whatsoever.

I finished work at 4 pm, home by 5 and ready to leave by 6.

"Does this look okay? I wasn't sure whether to wear my brown brogues or black?"

I wanted her approval on my outfit before we left, like any typical day. I always liked to have someone's opinion, and I knew she always liked what I wore; therefore, the answer would be the exact same as always.

"Yes, you look gorgeous. Brown was definitely the better choice."

This time her reply was disinterested. I could tell the prospect of the evening was still bothering her, so I made one last-ditch effort to make things better.

"Thank you, I thought so too. Are we okay? You know I love you, don't you?"

I walked behind her and put my arms around her waist as she stood statue-like in the mirror.

"I know you do, and I love you too. It just doesn't make me any less upset with you right now. Let's just leave it; you go out and have a good time."

"I'm sorry you are upset. You look beautiful if that's any consolation."

That was my way of sucking up; I had never been very good at it. Luckily for me, a cheeky smile or two got me out of most situations, although I think I had become a little too reliant on that.

"Yeah, whatever you say, suck up. We need to set off in a minute. Are you ready?"

"Just one last hair check, a spray of perfume and I am good to go."

I gave her a beaming smile before I sauntered off to the bathroom.

She shouted after me.

"So, what are you doing about your outfit anyway? Aren't you bothered about being the only one not dressed up?"

That thought had crossed my mind. Going to the meal meant I wouldn't have time to get back home and string together some form of an outfit that made me look even remotely scary. I also couldn't go to a posh restaurant covered in fake blood and looking like I'd been hit by a bus. The only realistic option was to go out not dressed up. It made me slightly disappointed because I was always the first to suggest an excellent fancy dress party. I hated people who refused to partake in anything like that. Where is the fun in that? Luckily for me, I had asked Paula earlier that day and she confirmed that I wasn't the only one not dressing up, so that made me feel a bit better. I would still have a good night, regardless.

"I won't be. I thought I might have been, but Paula said a few of the girls aren't dressing up. You know what they're like. How would they look good enough to pull a handsome, young man with all that blood on their face."

I rolled my eyes and couldn't help but laugh. I could picture their faces now, looking in disgust at the thought of dressing up. At the very most, they would've maybe worn a wig or a tail, but even that was doubtful.

"I can imagine. At least you won't be the only one then. Will it be a late one?"

"It will probably be the usual, babe. I will get a taxi with Paula, so don't worry about it."

The usual being no earlier than 3 am, sometimes even later if a takeaway was on the cards. I was excited just to go out: I could taste the alcohol.

I had one last outfit check before we left the house. My outfits never changed dramatically, and that night it was pretty simple; black skinny jeans, brown brogues and a black turtleneck jumper. The long sleeve was a must; the weather had dropped, and there was nothing worse than queuing to get into a night club in just a t-shirt. After some debate, I was happy with my outfit combination; it was time to leave.

We met Danielle's family at around 6:30 pm. The whole evening was based around her grandparents 50th wedding anniversary, but it also happened to be her sister's birthday the week after, so it was made into a joint celebration. I found it unbearable trying to make small talk with people I wasn't interested in talking to. Unfortunately for me, that is what most of the evening consisted of.

The table had been booked for 12 people at the Milano restaurant in the West End. It was a lovely Italian restaurant. I'd been several times and never once been disappointed with the food. The bonus being that it was only a ten-minute walk from where I needed to be afterwards.

I received a text at roughly 8 pm, a text I was surprised to see. It was from Brooke.

I hope you are coming out later. What time will you be here?

I hadn't heard anything from Brooke that day. She had been off work, so I was surprised, although I don't know why. I knew that she wanted me to go out, not for any particular reason, but I think she liked my company.

Of course, I am. I will be meeting Paula at Storm around 10. See you there?

Storm was probably the best nightclub in London, in my opinion. We would typically spend half our night in there, at least until it started to die off.

You will. See you later then.

I snapped back to reality when Danielle nudged me on the shoulder, hissing at me to put my phone away. It did look rather rude; I admit that. I put it in my pocket and continued the countdown—only an hour or so to go.

"It was lovely to see you too, Annette. Take care."

That was the final goodbye as Danielle walked me towards the door. Danielle and her family had decided they wanted to stay for a few drinks after the second bottle of rosé wine was brought to the table. That had been my cue to leave.

"Have a good night then. Text me when you get there and behave yourself."

"I will do, babe, you too. I'll try not to wake you when I get home. Love you."

"I love you too."

With that, I dashed off. The rain began to fall, which turned my walk into a speed walk then into a very light jog. The closer I got to the club, the more relieved I felt. I managed to make it without getting noticeably wet or, even worse, enduring a hair malfunction.

I spied Paula amongst all the dead-looking humans stood waiting to get inside. Her face lit up when she saw me hurrying towards her.

"You're here! I am so happy. I thought you might be late and I'd have to stand on my own with all the kids. You know I have no idea what they are talking about when they set off."

She called everyone a kid apart from me, even though most of our other colleagues were older than I was. Paula wasn't exactly up to date on technology so, when everyone started talking about Snapchat and Instagram, it was utterly lost on her. I admit, I was terrible for it myself, sometimes, but I think she was thankful to have a more mature head around her on a night out. That was up until we'd all had a few drinks, then I think she was probably the least mature out of us all.

"I wouldn't do that to you, would I? Is Lauren on her way?"

Lauren was a former lawyer who used to work with us at West & Hayes. Since the day she left, she had kept in contact with the majority of us. To be honest, a night out wasn't the same without her there. Lauren was the type of woman that could make a crowd full of mourners laugh; she should have been a comedian.

"I think she's already inside. I saw Brooke and her friends at the front of the queue when I arrived too. They couldn't squeeze me in with them though, that big man on the door wouldn't allow it."

It only took us five minutes to get inside. The dance floor and bar area were unbelievably busy, at least four people deep at the bar. From my experience, that was nothing new for a Friday night. It didn't take me long to spot Brooke in the corner of my eye. She looked my way and, for a second, our eyes locked; it was one of those moments that seem to last an eternity. I wasn't sure what to make of it at the time, but everything else faded away for those few seconds.

I was soon brought back to reality with a bit of help from a very drunk young woman and her swaying hand, which, of course, gripped an alcoholic drink that I no longer think she needed. It was just past 10 pm and, in my opinion, all she needed was her bed. Although I didn't appreciate the large Vodka and Coke spilt down my arm, there wasn't an awful lot I could do about it.

We made our way over to the rest of my colleagues who stood in the far corner. Slowly but surely, we pushed through the masses of people. I couldn't help but smile when I saw her up close. My eyes fixated on only her.

Why?

I had no idea.

CHAPTER FOUR

"Please tell me you aren't planning on queuing in that. Here have some of mine; it's not like I have a shortage."

My eyes had constantly been observing the bar, hoping it might die down. I was wrong; if anything, it proceeded to get busier. Brooke offered me a glass of her cocktail to ease the pain.

"Crazy, isn't it. It's a shame my friend isn't working; I could at least get served quicker. What on earth is that you're drinking?"

She shrugged her shoulders before taking another sip.

"I'm not entirely sure. I know it has Malibu in it and something strawberry and I think orange juice? It's nice; just have a glass."

I didn't have a choice in the matter. The glass was forced promptly into my hand, accompanied by a straw and what looked like unlimited ice cubes.

"Thank you. I will buy you one back when I can eventually get to the bar."

Cheers to that.

Three cocktails, two Sambuca shots and two Desperados later, the night was well underway. We moved on at around midnight, Penthouse being the next stop. It was more of an upper-class place, not too posh that they wouldn't cater for a bunch of drunken people in Halloween costumes, though. Cocktails were 2 for 1 (as always), which made them just under a fiver each; for Central London, that was a fantastic price.

I must admit, I enjoyed the view the most. The Penthouse was on the 7th floor of a 10-storey building, and it had a balcony that stretched around the outside. I could even see Big Ben from where I stood.

After an hour, I could see Paula feeling worse for wear, and I had already stopped her from falling over twice. I knew it was almost time to send for a taxi.

"Holly, you know I love you, and I think you are the best lawyer in London and the best friend I could wish for. I just wanted you to know I appreciate everything you do, and I love you. Did I tell you I love you?"

I couldn't help but laugh whilst trying to control her swaying body.

"Yes, Paula, at least five times already. I think it's time to get you home."

Paula's slurred words were rather hard to interpret amongst the music and the crowds of people.

"No, I won't let you leave when you are having such a good time. I'm not even that drunk."

"I'm going to call a taxi. You wait here and start saying your goodbyes."

It was 2 am so I wasn't upset about having to leave. It was my own choice, and I would generally get a taxi home with Paula on nights out because she only lived around the corner from me. Plus, I liked to make sure she got home safe. She was like another mum to me, one that seriously couldn't handle her alcohol, so I simply couldn't let her leave on her own. My night had been eventful enough anyway; I'd had plenty to drink and danced a few hours away, but I was ready to go home.

"You're leaving already?" a familiar voice shouted above the music.

"I know, I'm cutting it short tonight. I think someone needs to go home to bed."

I gestured towards Paula being propped up by Lauren.

"Yes, I can see that. It's been fun, though! I'll see you at work on Monday then?"

"You certainly will. Enjoy the rest of your night, Brooke. Don't do anything I wouldn't do."

There was a moment of awkwardness whilst we both weighed up the options. I had already hugged three people goodbye, and I wasn't sure if Brooke should be the fourth. After a few seconds of waiting, in a drunken haze, Brooke wrapped her arms around my neck and squeezed. It was sweet how she had to tiptoe slightly to reach. Even with high heels on, she was still slightly smaller. She had a big grin on her face when she finally let go.

"Goodbye, Holly."

"Goodbye, Brooke."

Monday morning came around, and I was back at work, just like that, as if I'd not just had two days off. That was always the case in my job. I needed time to unwind from the stresses of the job, so I would always look forward to my days off. Although they never were actual days off because I could guarantee, I would still receive numerous phone calls and emails. It was partly my fault for checking them, but I knew all too well from my first few years' experience that if you had two days off without checking your emails, you would regret it on Monday morning.

It did mean that I was never without my phone. If it wasn't a client calling, it was my boss; if it wasn't my boss, another lawyer wanted to talk through a case they were struggling with.

It was a fact that the higher and more respected you became in any walk of life, the less of a life you had. Luckily for me, it was a job I loved to do.

It was the 4th of November, and I walked into the office at 8 am to 15 new emails and four entries into the diary on my desk of people that I needed to call.

Many of the emails were leads in some of my cases; some were responses from clients, conference calls from Mr West that I needed to be on, amongst other things. Prioritising had to be a well-developed skill in my career to survive.

Every Monday morning, we would have a meeting in Room 101. This was a conference room purely for Mr West's use. I immediately pushed my laptop to one side and headed across to the other side of the floor.

"Morning, Holly."

"Morning, Mr West."

Usually, a chorus of greetings would come my way as I entered the room. It was significantly quieter that morning, with only three people present, those people being three people I knew very well; Paula, Brooke and Mr West.

"Thank you for being so prompt. I know you all have hectic days ahead of you, so I won't take up too much time. I have called you here today to discuss the Bickmore case."

Mr West handed us each a sheet of paper with the order of the meeting.

"This is a very high-profile case for us and I expect it will gather some momentum as we get closer to trial. I am already getting a lot of hassle from news media for details that we must not discuss at this stage. Holly, I assigned you this case because I knew you'd be the best person for the job. Brooke has glowing reviews from her time on the Family Law floor, so I think this would be a great and very challenging case to help out on. I am also giving you Paula; her depth of experience will help guide this case in the right direction and make sure we don't have any own goals. You two will report only to Holly regarding this case, and Holly, you will report only to me. Any challenges that arise, I want to hear about them immediately. Are we all okay with that?"

Mr West looked around the room for approval.

"Yes, crystal clear."

"Yes, Mr West."

"Sounds good."

There was a nod from each of us to accompany our words. I knew the case would be challenging, but I was confident in my ability to handle the most complex cases. Mr West had given me his most experienced paralegal and potentially his least experienced, but I could see the logic behind his thinking. Mr West rushed off, leaving us to discuss the case at hand.

Brooke looked confused for a second, and I couldn't help but notice the distant look on her face.

"Everything okay?"

She turned her head sharply towards me.

"Oh, yes, of course. I'm just thinking I like that coat the receptionist is wearing. I have wanted a coat just like that; I wonder where she got it from."

She was so serious. We had just been discussing a very high-profile, complex case, but Ashley's coat was what intrigued her most.

"Of course, you're thinking about Ashley's coat. Maybe you should go and ask her now because I understand how important that must be."

She smirked, as did I. Clearly, the sarcasm wasn't lost on her.

"Maybe, I will. I think I'll ask him to get it me for Christmas or my dad maybe. Yes, that's exactly what I'll do. Don't let me forget to ask her."

I glanced at Paula. She laughed, gathered her paperwork and promptly left.

As she left, she called out, "By him, I imagine you mean the boyfriend? What's his name again?"

She rolled her eyes before responding as if it pained her to talk about him.

"It's Luke. We aren't exactly on speaking terms at the minute, though, so I prefer to say 'him'."

Just mentioning his name seemed to make her uncomfortable so I didn't pry.

"Okay, well, I know this might be a little bit random, but I am free if you ever want to talk about it. I might be into women, but I did date boys back in school, so I have some idea of how incredibly obnoxious and annoying they are. I have been told my advice-giving isn't too bad either."

I totally made that up, of course. I am characteristically probably the most sarcastic person you will ever meet, but on the other hand, I was willing to give sound advice if she required it. I had also never dated boys unless you counted kissing Steven Saunders behind the bike sheds at school when I was 15. I may have even gone out with a young boy called Jack when I was 16 for a whole two weeks, but she didn't need to know that. For some reason, I just wanted her to feel comfortable like she could tell me anything. She smiled in return, and I took that as a sign that my sarcasm had been well received.

"I appreciate that. I may even take you up on the offer one day."

We shared a mutual smile that warmed my heart.

"Please do."

With that, I gathered my things and headed towards the door.

"Are you ready to get started?"

"Sure, just as soon as I have asked Ashley about that coat. I'll be right back."

Less than a minute later, I was back in my office perched on my brand-new, reclining, leather desk chair. The story with the chair was a rather interesting one. Basically, they sent the wrong one (not that interesting, I know), but they not only sent the wrong one once, they sent the wrong one twice. How you do that, I am not too sure. I would 100% be looking into the staff I employed if I was the boss. In the end, the company told me that I could keep the chair which, I might add, was £150 dearer than the hard-backed, boring office chair that I was due to receive. How they were so expensive anyway, I didn't understand.

I sat, rather smug, in my leather chair, as I now often did. Several emails later, Brooke returned. I didn't have to look up to know who it was as her perfume hit me before she even entered the room. I was so engrossed in the three-page email I was sending regarding an ongoing case that I was trying to wrap up. I knew I would need as much time as possible for the upcoming Bickmore case, which meant trying to tie up my other loose ends.

Although I sat comfortably in my role within West & Barnes, there was always someone above you, someone to answer to. That someone, for me, was Mr West. The number of hours I spent explaining the ins and outs of cases to him totted up to a considerable amount. One day, I hope to be in his shoes. My career goal is to own my own law firm, even if it only employed three lawyers. That, to me, is when I can sit back and feel like I have achieved something.

When no voice came from the silhouette stood at the door, I glanced up.

"I'm sorry. Do you want me to come back when you're ready to get started?"

She stood sheepishly in the doorway, like an intern on her first day. I suppose that's basically what she was.

"No, of course not. Just give me one second to send this email before I lose my train of thought. Take a seat, Brooke. I won't be a minute."

I typed away for another minute or two until I was satisfied, changed the subject line, made sure it was addressed to Mr West and then hit send.

"Sorry about that. I'm just trying to tie up a few loose ends. I have a lot going on at the minute, and now this case. More importantly, did you find out where Ashley's coat was from?"

We both laughed; she shook her head sadly.

"No, unfortunately, she seemed busy on the phone. I hung around for a minute but then realised I had some work to do. I'll catch her at dinner."

I raised both eyebrows in surprise.

"I have no doubt you will. Shall we get started? Let me find the information I gathered last week so we can get started with that. It should be here somewhere."

I searched through the piles of paperwork on my desk. I was an organised person – well, as organised as a lawyer could be when you have to juggle so many cases at once. Information needed to be readily available, even if that did make my desk look a little untidy and hard to navigate. When I finally located the file, I looked up to see Brooke looking towards the window, playing with her fingernails. She seemed nervous.

"Are you okay, Brooke? You seem a little apprehensive."

I could see she was unsure whether she wanted to tell me what was on her mind.

"I don't know. I feel like I want to talk to you, but I don't want to bore you with my problems. It's fine; let's just get to work."

I kept my gaze locked on her, and I could see her eyes starting to fill up. I instinctively stood up from behind my desk and walked around to the other side.

"Please, honestly, it's okay. I am all ears."

I could see she was struggling with the situation. I think, in some ways, she was very much like me. She didn't like to open up to anyone; she didn't want people to know just how down she was or how upset she might be. Maybe she needed a way she could let off some steam without causing a ripple effect.

"I don't know what to do anymore. I don't love Luke; at least, I don't think I do. All he does is bring me down. I don't think he means too; he isn't a terrible guy. He just doesn't treat me the way I would expect to be treated. He isn't bothered and he hasn't been for a long time, but then he blames me. It's me that doesn't try and it's me that's hard work. Whenever I tell him I'm not happy, he tries for a few days to make things better; then, it just goes back to normal. It's got to the point now where I don't even want to see him. We have a family wedding to go to next week and a birthday party the week after that. All these things planned, and we are expected to turn up as a couple, but I can't think of anything worse than spending time with him, pretending we are a happy couple when we are the furthest thing from it."

Brooke let out a big sigh of relief. It all came out in one long, rushed sentence, everything she had been holding in, punctuated with tears. I was never the best when it came to comforting someone. I wasn't an awful person. I just accepted, a long time ago, that I couldn't portray sympathy very well. I couldn't help but want to comfort her, anything to stop the tears from falling. Even me, who barely knew her, knew she didn't deserve to be upset like that.

"Come here, don't get upset. He isn't worth those tears."

I stood up from leaning against the desk and put my arm out, signalling a hug. She stood up, walked straight into my open arms, buried her head into my neck and wrapped her arms tight around my back. I didn't know what to do at first. The hug was slightly more intimate than I had intended it to be. Oddly enough, she fit into me like a glove. I wrapped my other arm around her back, and she squeezed, sobbing heavily as she did.

"It's okay; it will all be okay."

It honestly broke my heart to see her cry like that, to see her lost and unsure of what to do next. She was a mystery to me. At that time, I couldn't have even told you what car she drove, but what I did know is that the girl in my arms was fascinating. She was beautiful, she was kind-hearted and funny, and she was everything I wanted to get to know.

After a few minutes, Brooke wiped the tears from her face. I handed her a tissue from the desk and urged her to take a seat once again. I walked over to the door and closed it before we continued the conversation further. I wanted her to feel safe and secure. She was only human, after all, and it was normal to feel sadness.

"Thank you. I feel embarrassed that I've just stood here and basically cried to a stranger. You must think I'm insane."

"Well, you've met me on at least five different occasions now, I believe, so that makes me an acquaintance, not so much a stranger, so don't worry. You are far from insane. We have all been there, and you shouldn't be ashamed to get upset. It's not my place, but can I give you some advice?"

She didn't hesitate with her response.

"Sure. I'll take any advice I can get."

I didn't hold back.

"Your boyfriend, he sounds like a complete and utter asshole. Excuse my language. I can see it in the way you talk, that you love him. That's why it's difficult for you to realise that you may just be better off without him. All I can say is, talk to him properly. Sit down and tell him everything that bothers you and, if he walks away, if he blames you and makes no effort whatsoever to make things right, then you know he's not right for you. Then you know it's time to walk away. I have been there and done it. It's never easy, but life is too short to live it feeling the way you do now."

She smiled through the final tears, the tissue wiping away the last of them and leaving just the remnants of sadness.

"You are quite good at giving advice. I appreciate it. I feel a lot better already, just being able to get it off my chest. Anyway, maybe we should get on with some work; I don't want to give a bad impression to the lawyer I'm working with."

The sweet but sad smile she now sported was captivating.

"No, you don't want that. I have heard she can be a bit of a bitch."

I winked playfully.

"Really? I have a feeling that, once you get to know her, she is actually pretty alright. Thank you again, Holly."

The chemistry between us was palpable and something I hadn't been accustomed to for a long time.

"Anytime, Brooke."

She put the tear-stained tissue in the bin and looked up with a glowing smile. *'Back to putting on a brave face'*, I thought. I had a feeling that was something she was good at.

I got home later that night, Chinese takeaway in hand—a selection of Magic Wok's finest. My local Chinese takeaway was absolutely exquisite. I had been holding the bag for 5 minutes on the walk home, and I was practically drooling at the mouth. When I reached the front door, a sudden, anxious feeling came over me, as it often did when I thought of spending long periods of time there. I was never sure what sort of mood I would catch Danielle in. She was a difficult person to be around sometimes. She had started to suffer from depression a few years prior, and it often took over with nothing necessary to trigger it. I can't say it wasn't hard on our relationship.

"Dan? Are you home?"

There was no immediate answer when I entered, and I thought that maybe she was sleeping. All the lights were out apart from a flicker coming from underneath the bedroom door, indicating an array of candles must have been lit.

"Danielle, why didn't you answer me?"

She popped her head around the bathroom door.

"I'm sorry, babe, I didn't hear you. Can I smell Chinese?"

Her eyes lit up at the prospect of devouring the food.

"Yes, I got the usual. It's been a long day, so I figured takeaway was a good option."

"Sounds like an amazing option. I'll just finish up in here, then you can tell me about your day."

"Okay, I'll plate it up ready."

I tried to sound somewhat engaged, but my mind always wandered. It had gotten to the stage in my relationship where I valued my alone time. As awful as it might sound, I enjoyed it when Danielle went to bed early or visited family for the evening. It meant I could do as I pleased; I didn't have to make small talk or pretend to be interested in some aspect of her job that I had no interest in.

Did that make me a bad person? I often asked myself that very question.

"Smells delicious. Can we stay up and watch a film tonight?"

Danielle entered the kitchen.

"Sure, what are you thinking? As long as it's some terrible, scary film that is so unrealistic that I want to write a letter to the director. What was the last one you made me watch again?"

She laughed. I always had a rant about terrible horror movies, but she still insisted I watch them, always telling me I would enjoy the next one.

"I think it was called the Wrong Turn, wasn't it? Okay, so no scary film then. I will let you choose for a change. How's that?"

"Sounds perfect to me."

There was only one movie genre I was choosing from, and that was a comedy, with the occasional rom-com thrown into the mix.

The food was terrific, as it always was. It took me 5-10 minutes to devour every last bit. I cleared away the plates and empty takeaway containers before settling down on the sofa next to Danielle. Before I had the chance to get comfortable, she immediately fired a question my way.

"Who's Brooke?"

"Huh?"

I didn't know how to respond to the question at first. Why was she asking me that?

"Your phone flashed whilst you were in the kitchen. You have a text from Brooke. You've never mentioned a Brooke, so I was just wondering who it was."

I found it hard to believe that I hadn't mentioned her, but it was plausible given how little I talked about my work life to Danielle. I always gave her the short, watered-down version of my days.

"Oh, okay, I was confused for a second. Brooke is one of the new paralegals at work; haven't I mentioned her? She only came onto the team the week before last."

I felt a pang of guilt, but I wasn't sure why.

"Nope, I don't recall you mentioning her. Why are you texting her though?"

The message from Brooke was a welcome surprise. I had no idea what the message would contain because I hadn't spoken to her via text at all that day.

"I'm not sure why she's text. It will just be about work. She left me her number the other week so that I could contact her about a case we are working on."

There was a clear look of confusion and uncertainty upon Danielle's face. She had always been a very jealous person, but only recently had she gotten so outrageously unreasonable. It had become the cause of 90% of our arguments. I went back to looking at the list of films on the television, waiting for her to continue the conversation like I knew she would.

"So, aren't you going to reply?"

The pressure was building.

"I'm going to have a look in a second."

I opened the text message, and it simply read:

Thank you so much for today. It meant a lot. B x

A smile crept upon my face, short and sweet. It filled me with satisfaction to know that I had been of help at a time when she had needed someone to talk to. I hoped Danielle wouldn't see it as anything more than that, but she assumed every girl I spoke to had an ulterior motive and, granted, some girls did.

I don't believe Brooke was one of those girls, so I showed Danielle the text, knowing that's what she was waiting for.

"What does she mean? Thank you for what?"

"She came into the office crying today, troubles with her boyfriend. I just gave her some advice, that's all."

She didn't take her eyes off me for about 30 seconds, looking for some trace of the lie that wasn't there.

"And what qualifies you for giving boyfriend advice? All of that personal experience?"

She was trying to make light of the situation after realising that I had nothing to hide.

"Are you saying my kiss with Steven wasn't an experience? Because I remember how disgusting that kiss was. Anyway, I don't need to have been in a heterosexual relationship to give advice about boys. It was just general advice. Even you say I think like a man most of the time, so I guess I am well equipped to offer words of wisdom."

She laughed, probably at the idea of my teenage self.

"I believe you. You always know the right thing to say in situations like that."

I took that as an opportunity to change the subject.

"Anyway, let's get this film on. What about this comedy? No, wait, this one looks better…Ohhh, this one is so funny."

The debate with myself continued for a few minutes until I settled on Happy Gilmore - if ever in doubt, put on an Adam Sandler film, always a certified winner. I sent a concise reply to Brooke, just to acknowledge I had read the message. I didn't like to ignore people, and I felt almost compelled to reply, like, if I didn't, I'd be offending her. I didn't want that.

Not a problem, Brooke. You know where I am if you ever need to talk.

There was no reply after that. I spent the rest of the evening curled up on the sofa with Danielle. Just like any other night, it was relaxing, nothing out of the ordinary. My life was simply comfortable, and I wasn't sure how I felt about that.

The next day was the 5th November, bonfire night. It was such a spectacular evening, one night of the year, when the whole sky lights up in unison. In my experience, bonfire night had always been a rather wet and cold affair. Every year, I would complain that I couldn't feel my feet or my hands were going to drop off, and my hair was wet. I did exaggerate slightly sometimes. I wasn't soft when it came to anything, apart from being cold; that was the one thing I absolutely hated. I should have been born abroad, the summer sun beating down on me every day and a constant glowing natural tan—no more cold England.

One day maybe.

There was still something about bonfire night that made my stomach tighten. I'd had a near miss as a child, although I don't remember much of it now, I just remember standing in front of a bonfire that my father's friend had started.

The flames must have been 6 feet off the ground, but it was something we did every year, so it was always controlled. The local neighbours would come around, some family and friends, and everybody would chip in for fireworks and food. It was always a great night.

That year was slightly different, though. My cousin and his friends, who were seventeen at the time, decided it would be a good idea to throw a bunch of fireworks onto the bonfire when nobody was looking. The fireworks shot off in every direction, most people managed to get out of the way, but several got hit, including myself. One of the fireworks flew past my head, inches from my ear, burning the side of my face and partially deafening me in the process. My hearing came back almost fully but, even to this day, I feel like my hearing is not quite as clear as it should be.

I think back now at how lucky I was: A few inches to the right, and it could have taken my eye out completely. After that ordeal, the garden bonfires stopped, and in the years that followed, we opted for a professionally supervised event.

That year, we had decided upon the Alexandra Palace Firework Festival. Danielle and I had been for the past two years, and we couldn't fault it. There was so much to do, from food stalls to fairground rides. The bonfire would always start around 6 pm, and the firework display would follow at 8 pm.

I received a text message from Danielle at around noon that day.

I don't know if going out tonight is a good idea. I can't leave Sunny on her own. She was cowering all night last night with the fireworks, and they're only going to be worse tonight. I feel sorry for her, babe. You know how much I love her. If your friends are still going, I don't mind if you go and meet them. I'll just stay at home by myself.

Sunny was Danielle's dog. She was nine years old and the softest, most loving thing you could imagine. She was an English Springer Spaniel, brown and white with huge ears that could wrap around her whole head. She was the love of Danielle's life, and I was often told that I shared this role with Sunny. That suited me just fine because I had grown up surrounded by dogs. I think I enjoy their company a little more than I did people.

I had almost pre-empted the situation if I am totally honest. The text message was typical for Danielle, always saying one thing but meaning another. It was clear to me that if I still went to the bonfire, an argument would follow. Even though she clearly stated that she didn't mind if I went, that was her way of trying to appear reasonable. There was no doubt in my mind that I would be going to the bonfire at Alexandra Palace. The only question was, who would I be going with?

I quickly typed up a reply.

I had a feeling you would want to stay in with Sunny after last night. I think I will still go and meet some friends from work if that's okay. I already told them we are going. At least one of us should make an appearance. I won't stay out too late.

I received a short reply, *'OK'*. There was one thing Danielle knew about me; I would always do what I wanted to do. I considered her feelings, but by that point, she knew how much I wanted to go out.

I loved to socialise, it was one thing I was very good at, and networking was always something that had been drilled into me from a young age. My father would always tell me: *'If you want to get somewhere in life, you need to befriend the right people, never burn your bridges'*. I believe that is the reason I grew up to be such a smooth talker. I could convince almost anyone of anything; it was a gift. It was the reason I had done so well in my career, the reason I had secured the most excellent apartment on my block for the lowest price. For as long as I could remember, getting my own way had been second nature.

Paula walked in and disturbed my train of thought.

"Holly, I have a problem."

"What is it, Paula?"

"Jeremy won't come to the bonfire with me tonight. I won't get into the whole reason why, but he's just a complete ass. So, I have no way of getting there to meet you and Danielle."

How unreasonable of me to think it might have been something about the case. Jeremy was Paula's on-and-off boyfriend at the time. She had been married to a guy called

James for ten years, but they got divorced three years ago; shortly after that, she met Jeremy, who was eight years her junior. I had met him a couple of times, and he seemed slightly arrogant, a bit chauvinistic, but Paula seemed to like him. Well, when he wasn't an ass, that was.

"Funny you should say that. Danielle isn't coming either. She's staying in with Sunny. So, how about we get off a little early today, and I'll pick you up around 5:30, so we can go together?"

It wasn't often I would finish early, but I thought I owed myself the luxury of attending significant events throughout the year. I would think of it as my treat for all the late nights and weekends checking emails.

"That sounds perfect."

"Problem solved."

I spent a lot of time with Paula outside of work. She was a lot older than I was, but that didn't take away from the fact she was hilarious to be around and, undoubtedly, one of my closest friends.

The rest of the day went as smoothly as I could've hoped for; I managed to get off work just after 4 pm. I had roughly an hour to get home, get changed and head back out to pick up Paula. I certainly did not have time to be arguing with Danielle. She was reasonable - most of the time - rarely would she cause a huge scene. Instead, she would be silent and I think that was a lot worse. It was sometimes difficult to tell just how long she would be pondering for. I could be in the bad books for a day, a week, a month, I never knew.

I arrived home just before 5 pm. I quickly changed my jeans from a black pair to blue and threw my white shirt straight into the wash, exchanging it for a grey jumper. I took one look in the mirror, touched up my hair and makeup by applying a very thin layer of foundation. I had to dig out my Hunter wellies from the back of my wardrobe. I had two pairs; both purchased several years ago, both looked brand new. They only ever made an appearance on bonfire night and the occasional day during winter when we had a decent level of snow.

I sent Danielle a quick text message before I left the house.

Sunny's fed and watered, fireworks aren't bad around here at the minute, so she's okay. I am just leaving to go and pick Paula up now. I don't want to miss the bonfire. I hope you've had a nice day at work. See you tonight. I love you. x

It only took me 10 minutes to get to Paula's house in Holborn, and it was about a 30-minute drive from there to Alexandra Palace. It was a lot easier to get there by car than it was to catch several underground trains.

Sometimes, it felt like a waste having a car, trying to drive around Central London was not worth the hassle, so I would catch the underground most of the time. My car was a company car, so it didn't matter much to me whether it sat at home all day: I didn't pay for it, and the company were even kind enough to pay for my train expenses, knowing full well the car was sat at home barely being used. It was there if I ever needed it and that I was grateful for.

I guess my job had its perks.

The drive was one of many laughs, as it always was in Paula's company. We bounced off one another; nobody could say the things we say to each other and get away with it.

It felt like a mere five minutes had passed when we pulled up to the nearby car park.

The place was hectic and from what I could see, the bonfire hadn't started, but the queue to get anywhere close was incredibly long. With most people distracted by the crowd, we found the nearest, most convenient place to grab a drink.

"I didn't expect it to be this busy, Holly."

"It was like this last year too. It doesn't seem to quieten off either. Even after the fireworks, people still wander around and have some drinks and food. It's a nice atmosphere, though; you will enjoy it."

Paula did complain a lot, but it was probably her only downfall. If she weren't complaining, she would be panicking, and if she wasn't panicking, then something was wrong.

"I'm sure I will. Anyway, what are you having to drink? I'll get these."

Paula pulled a small, red purse from her black, cross-body bag.

"Just grab me a Coke, if you don't mind. I can't have any alcohol, can I."

I gestured towards the car keys bulging out of my front pocket.

"I can get them to stick a bit of Vodka in that Coke, and we can leave the car here. What do you say?"

She was raising her eyebrows in the most unconvincing, creepy way. I tried to contain it, but I burst out laughing.

"What and catch the dreaded underground? No thanks. We won't get home until this time next week. It will be insanely busy."

No doubt a good percentage of the thousands of people at the event would be catching the underground home, and that wasn't something I wanted to be involved in.

"That's a slight exaggeration but okay, Hol. Whatever you say. I'm sure I can drink your Vodka as well as my own."

I shook my head.

"You have work at eight and we have a lot to do, so that's a huge no from me."

Her face spoke a thousand words.

"When did you become so bossy?"

"Since I met you. Someone needs to keep you in check."

We both laughed.

"That is a very valid point. I love how I am old enough to be your mother, but it's you that tells me what to do."

It worked well for us both, despite the constant complaints. Paula finally got served at the bar after ten minutes of deliberating what she wanted to drink.

The bonfire was due to start any minute, so we made our way through the crowds of people. There was plenty of room towards the front, but it was getting there that proved the hard part. We settled a few rows back, with about three people between me and the bonfire, but the sightline was slightly obscured by the giant of a man stood at the front. I was a decent 5'8", so I'm almost positive he must have been 6'5".

"You may have to get me on your shoulders soon, Paula."

She pulled a disgruntled face at the several people in front of her that were also significantly taller than she was, but that wasn't difficult.

"When did we start living in a world full of giants? Half of the children here are taller than me; it's ridiculous."

I just laughed to myself while awkwardly turning my head in every direction, trying to find the best angle.

All of a sudden, I heard a loud shriek to my left. I turned quickly to find a man, not much taller than myself, with his arms wrapped around Paula's waist, pulling her in playfully. It took me a moment to register that it was Jeremy. Paula's face was not finding the situation quite as entertaining as he was.

Jeremy looked different from the last time I saw him. A well-grown, black beard with speckles of grey now covered a large amount of his face, and his jacket looked a little tighter around the waist. Paula did feed him enough in a day to last him a week, so it was no surprise that he was putting on a bit of weight.

It was his eyes that caught me. As he looked towards me and smiled, his eyes appeared drawn and tired. Maybe it was stress at work? He was always at work, from what Paula told me, and it seemed like his job demanded ninety percent of his time.

"Jeremy, what on earth are you doing here?"

"I came to surprise you, sweetheart. I got off work a few hours earlier than expected. Aren't you happy to see me?"

Paula looked far from happy.

"I would've been happy to see you last night, but you never came home, so no, I'm not exactly over the moon right now."

Paula removed his arms from around her waist and continued to watch the bonfire. The stress from Jeremy's job caused most arguments between them. It had brought a rift between them both for the past year, and I often wondered if it were something they would ever be able to move past.

"There's no need to be like that with me, Paula. I thought I was doing a nice thing. I thought you'd want to spend the evening with me. Honestly, you drive me insane. I can't win with you."

Jeremy nodded towards me before he took off: An apologetic nod, I imagine, for me having to witness one of their arguments, yet again. What shocked me was how unaffected they were by doing it in public.

I looked towards Paula, counting to five in my head before she turned towards me.

"I should go after him, shouldn't I? I'm sorry, Hol. Are you going to be okay?"

'A bonfire night for one,' I thought.

"Yes, you should. Go and sort it out. He obviously just wanted to surprise you. I'll be fine; I can manage on my own."

She gave me a sympathetic hand squeeze before rushing off. I did feel like a bit of a loner; I stood and watched the bonfire for the next ten minutes alone with no sign of Jeremy or Paula.

Jeremy would have driven to the event, so I anticipated a phone call or a text message, at some point, telling me they had gone home to sort things out. I felt like it was my time to leave: I didn't fancy staying and watching the fireworks all on my own; there wasn't much fun in that. Besides, I could be seen by anyone at Alexandra Palace, and there was no way I wanted anyone taking pity on me for my lack of company.

I gave it twenty minutes before I turned to leave. I weaved my way through a group of teenagers, a family with three screaming children and several young couples before I found myself confronted with a familiar face.

I was about to excuse myself kindly so I could squeeze past, but I saw the purple wellies and looked up.

Of all the people to be stood directly in front of me, probably the one person that, for some reason, I did not want to look like a loser in front of.

Yes, it was Brooke.

CHAPTER FIVE

"Not leaving already, are you?"

I stared at the face in front of me for what felt like hours until I finally managed to open my mouth and conjure up a reply.

"I was thinking about it. Are you here on your own?"

There didn't seem to be anyone stood around her, prompting my quick observations.

"No, I came with a few of my friends. I thought it was you I saw earlier. Where's Paula gone?"

"Paula had a few things to sort out."

I wasn't about to delve into personal information about Paula that didn't concern Brooke. There was a brief silence as we stared at one another, except it wasn't awkward, and I couldn't put my finger on why.

"Well, I'm going to go and find a good spot for the fireworks. Want to come along?"

I glanced over towards a group of girls looking our way and they quickly turned their backs towards us.

"What about your friends?"

I wondered if she felt sorry for me and that was the only reason she asked.

"They can find me later; they are more bothered about attracting all the single boys. I, on the other hand, actually want to watch the firework display, so feel free to join me."

She took off through the crowd; there was no waiting for my reply. I think that she assumed I would follow, so I didn't want to disappoint. I had been looking forward to watching the fireworks. I probably would've stayed to watch them, even if I hadn't bumped into Brooke. At least, that's what I told myself. I was suddenly no longer concerned with Paula's antics.

We found the perfect spot where only a group of ten-year-old children separated us from the barriers and the clear signs, stating we must not go closer.

"Here is okay, right? They should be starting any minute."

Brooke turned back, looking for approval.

"Looks great to me. You really know how to move through a crowd, don't you? I almost lost you for a second."

"Well, I got us to the front, didn't I? There's no point coming to watch the fireworks if you're stood behind the big, friendly giant over there."

We both laughed: She had a good point. If there was one thing I noticed about Brooke, it was her wittiness. There was an underlying sarcasm, always prepared to come out with the following comment. I liked that about her, the fact that she wasn't afraid to have a joke at her own expense.

"Fair enough. I bow to your crowd manoeuvring greatness."

I could see her smiling from the corner of my eye as I looked towards the trees, eagerly waiting for the fireworks to start.

"You are more sarcastic than me; I like that."

I swear I saw her wink, but it was dark, so I couldn't be 100% sure.

"Yeah? We agree on something then."

Brooke nudged me playfully.

"I think we do."

The night sky erupted above us with the crackling of fireworks. Explosions of colour from every angle lit up the atmosphere. So many sounds of amazement from the children enveloped us; even the adults failed to hold in the excitement. Bonfire night was indeed a magical night, even with the gentle drops of water falling around me and my feet sinking into the damp, dirt-ridden field. There was still something about how it made you feel.

It brought people together, families, and groups of friends, cuddling, laughing, and joking as they raised their heads towards the black night sky.

At that moment, I looked to my left at the sweet innocence on Brooke's face. It was almost like that of a child, a child that had yet to experience the worst of the world. It was somewhat compelling, endearing. I couldn't tear my eyes away, and the fireworks almost faded into the background as my mind became preoccupied entirely. There was a split second when I knew she caught me staring; I turned my head away instantly to avoid being too obvious.

"Amazing, aren't they?"

We both stared in awe as the last part of the fireworks started to erupt. There was always the big finale and I wondered how they would outdo themselves yet again.

"Incredible, even better than last year."

"I didn't come here last year; I went to a friend's house party. It was good but, as you can imagine, not quite comparable to this."

"Well, at least you've experienced it this year."

I had a sudden urge to ask a question, but I wasn't sure how it would be received.

"Can I ask you a question, Brooke?"

She turned away from the fireworks as they came to a close to give me her full attention.

"Of course, Holly. What is it?"

"If you felt like you weren't happy, would you do something about it? Or would you just carry on because it's the easiest thing to do?"

I know she was questioning what I could be referring too. Maybe I had overstepped the boundary slightly. I rarely discussed my personal life and never with someone that wasn't in my immediate circle. There was something about her that made me want to tell her, made me want to find out her opinion as if I would somehow value it more than my own. That was very unusual to me when someone has that quiet, calmness about them: It almost pulls you in, it intrigues you and makes you feel like you can confide in them. Brooke had that quality about her.

"That depends what you are talking about, a relationship? Or work, maybe?"

Her prying eyes never once left mine.

"Neither. It doesn't matter; forget I asked."

"Don't do that. You can tell me, you know. You obviously had something on your mind. I won't tell anyone if that's what you're worried about."

I saw the sincerity in her eyes and I believed she was someone that I could confide in; that was enough for me.

"A relationship – well, my relationship, to be precise. I don't even know why I feel the urge to tell you. I was just thinking about how Danielle should have been here with me tonight, watching these fireworks. The sad thing is, I'm relieved that she isn't. What does that tell you?"

There was a slight pause before another eruption of fireworks as they ramped up into the final stage before the epic finale. Even though everything around us was so loud, I could hear every word she was saying.

"That tells me that you may be unsure of what it is you want. You guys have been together a long time, right? Maybe you need to get the spark back. Maybe it will just take a little bit of time. Sit down and have a talk with her, tell her how you feel. You were happy once, so you can be happy again, surely."

She was sincere when she spoke.

"I don't know; maybe it's too late for that. If you're meant to be with someone, shouldn't you always be happy? I know everyone argues, and I know disagreements are a part of life, but we don't argue. That's not what makes me unhappy."

Brooke's facial expression changed to one of confusion. She leaned in closer as she asked the next question.

"Then what is it, Holly? What makes you so unhappy?"

That was the million-dollar question.

"The truth? I don't think I am in love with her anymore. I think I fell out of love a long time ago and I've been trying to get it back ever since, but it hasn't worked. I've tried everything and now I'm unhappy. I stay at work late so I don't have to go home and endure the same conversations and the same routines. I'm unhappy, mostly because I know how much she loves me, and I don't want to break her heart."

There was an understanding between us in that moment. She saw exactly where I was coming from and I think she could connect with me on that level because she, too, found herself in a situation where she was no longer happy.

"You gave me some great advice when I needed it, so I feel as though I should return the favour. I know what it's like to feel unhappy, but at the same time, you remember when you were happy and you fight for that; you fight to get back to what once felt so right. You continue to try even though, deep down, you are wasting your time because, once it's gone, you have lost half the battle. Only you know how you feel, and only you know when the time is right to let go."

"You are right." I said.

"I know I am. Someone told me something very similar once, and she was right too."

Just as the last word exited her mouth, an overwhelming brightness erupted over the whole of London. I had never seen anything quite like it; an array of colours, patterns and sounds that managed to merge into one enormous display that took the crowd by surprise.

My favourite was the very end, where I thought the last firework had malfunctioned somehow when nothing happened straight away. Then three bangs came one after another, and the sky spelt out *'HAPPY BONFIRE NIGHT'*. The firework finale was one to remember.

I dread to think how much it cost to put something like that together. With the entry fee being as little as £3, I can't see how they made their money back but, year in, year out, they continued with the most dramatic firework displays. They certainly never failed to disappoint me.

"I enjoyed that. I will definitely be coming here next year."

"I always say I will try somewhere different, but it's my fourth year in a row coming here. Why go somewhere else when it's so good?" I replied.

We both smiled in silent agreement. There wasn't much else to say after that, and I knew she would be going back to her friends. I would be heading home early, much to my disappointment. I'd had an evening of food and laughter planned with Paula, plans which were now very much off the cards.

"So, I guess I will see you at work tomorrow? I'll let you get back to your friends. Thanks for taking pity on me and watching the fireworks."

We both laughed.

"I didn't take pity on you. Believe it or not, I enjoy your company. It's nice to actually talk to someone and not just about getting drunk or having sex with boys. My friends are slightly immature. I will see you tomorrow then."

"It's fine, honestly. I love a good pity party. See you around, Brooke."

I walked away, only looking back to give her a cheeky wink so that she knew I was joking. Her response was the most beautiful smile I think I had ever seen. It was a genuine, kind-hearted smile, one that could melt your heart in an instant.

I left Alexandra Palace feeling uplifted. What could have been a disastrous evening turned out to be one I would remember. It was short and sweet, but it stuck with me the whole drive home and on into the night.

Have you ever met someone and instantly felt like you had known them your whole life? One or two conversations, and you feel like you could tell them anything. It's a strange feeling and not one everyone will experience. That person will, more than likely, turn out to be your best friend or, possibly, the love of your life; in the luckiest circumstances, they may even be both.

I didn't hold much hope for that at the time. I knew there was something about Brooke and the more I spoke with her, the more I realised just how much we had in common.

I was intrigued to find out more about her life. What made her happy? What she did outside of work? Was she close to her family? Where had she been on holiday? What was her dream job? You name it; I wanted to know it.

She was fascinating to me. As the days went by, I found myself engulfed in the most random conversations with her. Neither one of us questioned why we spoke as much or why we found it so easy to get along.

I can't speak for her, but she slowly became the highlight of my day. When you have the same routine, day in day out, week after week, year after year, it becomes repetitive. You look for some new source of entertainment, something to spice up your day. With my home life not quite where I would have liked it to be, I needed that, a distraction. She was that for me; she became the ultimate distraction.

It was now the 15th of November, and winter was really starting to settle in. The first signs of snow had appeared several nights before. I dreaded the snow and, if you lived in England, it was nothing but a huge inconvenience. The country practically shut down and the firm became very quiet with the cancellation of face to face appointments. The streets were almost deserted as anyone that could stay at home chose to do so.

Unfortunately for me, I could still get to work, so I did not have the privilege of sitting at home by the fire. To be completely honest, I preferred to go to work. It meant I had no distractions and I focused more in that environment.

Snow had fallen again that morning, and as much as I preferred fresh snow to ice, I did not care for the children throwing snowballs on my journey to work. Schools all over the country had closed and called a snow day, meaning the kids had nothing to do but have fun. If only it were the same for adults.

There had only been me and four other colleagues able to get in that day from our floor, one of those being Brooke. One saving grace with days like that: It gave me the perfect opportunity to catch up on the endless amount of paperwork on my desk.

I knew most of my appointments that day would have been cancelled, which bought me more time to close out on some other cases and continue with the ever-growing Bickmore case. My phone, however, was ringing off the hook so, by noon, Ashley had to prioritise the calls and take messages for the majority. The halls felt like a ghost town, but it was nice to have some calm. I could see the snow building up outside and wondered how I would get home if it continued.

It got to just after 1 pm when there was a knock at the office door. My heart sank when I looked up to see that it wasn't Brooke.

"Holly, sorry to bother you. The snow is getting quite bad, and my dad asked me to ring him if it got any worse because he won't be able to pick me up if it continues. Is there any possibility of me leaving early? You're the senior in today."

I took a quick glance out of the window. The snow was coming down thick and fast. I rechecked the weather app, and there didn't seem to be any sign of it easing off.

"Of course, Amy, I don't want you getting stuck here. Give your dad a ring. I'm sure you can pick up some work from home anyway, can't you?"

She smiled and nodded in agreement.

"Okay, thanks, Holly. I will go and let him know."

I quickly dialled through to Ashley at reception. "Hi, Holly."

"Hi, Ash. Amy is going early. It's getting pretty bad out there, and you know how far away she lives. Will you get Mr West on the phone for me? I think it's best we all think about leaving early."

"Not a problem, Holly. I'll try and get through to him now."

A few minutes later and the phone began to ring.

"I have Mr West on line three for you, Holly."

"Thanks, Ash."

I picked up the call and Mr West immediately spoke.

"Holly, why are you still at work? The snow is getting terribly deep. Will you make sure that everyone leaves and gets home safely before you all end up camping out in my corridors."

Great minds think alike, I guess.

"Mr West, I was just calling to ask if that would be alright. It doesn't seem to be easing up like I thought it would."

"Yes, I think that's wise. I appreciate you making an effort to get in when others couldn't, but you needn't have. You can do most of your work from home so work the next few days from there if it doesn't clear up. Just advise the rest of the team to do the same, please. I am still available via the phone or email if they need anything."

I knew what his answer would have been, but it didn't hurt to ask. We quickly said our goodbyes, and I turned to my computer to compose an email, informing the rest of the building that everyone was to go home before the snow prevented us from doing so.

I hit the send button and began to gather my things.

I was the only one with keys which meant, unfortunately, I had to wait until everyone had exited the building before I could leave. Most people went promptly whilst others must have been finishing up on phone calls. The clock seemed to be no longer ticking, and what felt like an hour had only been twenty minutes.

Amy's dad had been prompt in picking her up; the snow almost looked like it would subside. As soon as that thought crossed my mind, it seemed to pick up again and snowflakes the size of my hand began to shower down over the whole of London. At one point, it became a worry that we may get snowed in, which had never happened before in my lifetime. I can't imagine there ever being enough snow in England to warrant me not leaving the house or, in that case, the firm.

I went back to recheck the computer, making sure I had no replies. I was waiting for the all-clear, so I knew my fellow colleagues had left the building.

I went out into the corridor to find Brooke.

"How's it going? Did you do a sweep?"

"Yes, I can't see anyone else on our floor. Ashley just left. Any news from the others?"

"I am just waiting on Darren and Sarah from the third floor, but I may have to go and clear them out myself. I can't be waiting any longer now. I don't fancy sleeping here tonight."

Brooke nodded.

"Let's get our things and head to the third floor then. We need to get home safely too."

"I agree. Give me 2 minutes to get my things, and I'll meet you at the lift."

I closed my laptop down and placed it in my briefcase with another ten files that needed urgent attention: They would keep me busy for the next few days. Once I reached the lift, Brooke was eager to leave.

"I could murder a cappuccino or a hot chocolate right now. That's the one thing this place lacks, a decent coffee machine. You would think they'd have one, being one of the best law firms in the city, wouldn't you?"

She rolled her eyes as we entered the lift and I couldn't help but laugh.

"Well, maybe you should suggest that to Mr West. The one we have is a little outdated. I would maybe give it a tad longer, though, before you start slagging off his coffee machine. Get your feet under the table first."

She smirked, knowing full well that I was right.

"Can't you mention it? He loves you. I'm sure you could charm him into adding a swanky, new Barista Pro or something."

I side-eyed her as if to say, *'yeah, right'.*

"A Barista Pro? I'm sure they're about £800. You've got more chance of him buying the Starbucks down the road. Which brings me nicely to: Why don't you grab one on your way home?"

Her eyes lit up as if it wasn't something she had even considered.

"That sounds like a great idea. Why don't you join me? I'd rather have someone to walk to the station with, just in case I fall over and break my ankle or something."

"Look, you don't have to pretend you are in danger of breaking your ankle to spend more time with me, you know."

She knew that I wasn't serious. Anyone that knew me knew how much of a wind up I was. I had grown fond of teasing her in particular - I thrived off it. The banter that bounced between us when we were together was electrifying. She elbowed me playfully.

"You are such an idiot, Holly. Do you want a Starbucks or not?"

I smiled.

"A Starbucks sounds amazing right now."

As we touched down on Level 3, Darren and Sarah were ready to enter the lift: It couldn't have been more perfect timing.

It was just after 2 pm when we left the building. The outside air hit me like a ton of bricks, but there was six inches of snow on the ground, so, of course, it was going to be cold. As wrapped up as I was, I was not prepared for the sheer bitterness of the wind that day and, within seconds of being outside, my face felt almost numb. I pulled up my collar and wrapped my knitted, grey snood up around my face to try and keep the cold at bay. We swiftly made our way towards the end of the road.

"I think we need to get to Starbucks before we freeze to death. It's ridiculous out here."

Brooke was slightly less prepared for the cold weather. Other than her wellies, she wore an outfit suited for a warm summer's day, not the freezing winter.

"I agree. I see you were prepared for the weather this morning. Don't you own warm clothing?"

"Actually, yes, I do, thank you. I was just in a rush this morning, and I didn't realise it was going to resemble the North Pole out here, did I."

I laughed at her attitude. The way she pronounced certain words amused me, and I almost wanted to ask her to repeat things. I thought that might be strange, so I refrained.

"Did the snow not give it away? That would've been a pretty clear indication, but maybe that's just me."

"Oh, is that what that white stuff is? Silly me."

The witty banter between us continued until we reached the coffee shop. We couldn't get inside quick enough; my nose had already turned red. If it had been a month later, I could have passed for Rudolph.

The coffee shop was almost deserted, except for an elderly couple to the far right and two business people on the left, savouring every last drop of their coffee before venturing out into the cold again. As we entered, a staff member placed a sign on the door saying, 'REDUCED OPENING HOURS, THIS STORE WILL CLOSE AT 4 PM DUE TO BAD WEATHER'.

That gave us plenty of time.

We both ordered a hot chocolate with marshmallows and whipped cream. The baristas presented them in such a way that made my mouth drool. Of course, we both wanted the same drink, but I could have predicted that before we even entered the coffee shop. We took the table nearest to the window so that we could look out at the snow.

Just as we sat down, the manager came out and informed us all that they would be closing at 4 pm, as the sign stated.

"Isn't it funny how nobody can deal with snow over here? I went to America in the winter a few years back, and I thought that I'd be stranded, that planes wouldn't be flying, and cars wouldn't be on the roads. None of that! They just got on with it; everything was open like any other normal day." I said.

"Where did you go to in America?"

"To Chicago. One of my old friends from school moved over there when she was about fourteen. I've been over a few times to see her. It's such a great place, Brooke. Have you ever been?"

"I went to Florida when I was little but not recently. I would love to go back, though, do a full tour of all the states. Miami or New York would have to be the first stop for me. They just look incredible."

"New York is amazing; I went there for a few days last year. I was in awe the whole time; it's like a different world. You have to be able to move with the crowds, though. If you get stressed out in busy places, it's not the place for you."

I could tell she was intrigued. Most things I said seemed to interest her, which I liked.

"Is it as busy as it looks? Like, on the films and stuff? Does everyone wear suits and talk into their phone?"

"Sometimes it's busier. You just have to remember that most people are going about their daily routine. There are many businessmen and women so yes, a lot of suits and a lot of tourists. It's fascinating to watch. If you ever go, just sit down on a bench somewhere and watch the people go by.

You'd be fine, though. You're from London, so you are already used to the crowds."

"Yeah, that's true. One of my friends went a couple of years ago, and she said it was just like London on steroids. I'm adding the tour of America to my bucket list. Do you have a bucket list?"

"I didn't think people actually did those. Do you actually have a list? Like, you've written it down?"

I knew people spoke about adding something to their bucket list if there was something they just had to do, but I didn't know anyone that had actually written it down. I thought, if anything, it was a figure of speech.

"Of course, I have. How else would I remember all the amazing things I want to do before I die?"

"Okay, this is interesting. What is on this list of yours?"

"Let me think…Okay, swimming with dolphins is definitely on there - if that's not on everyone's bucket list, then something's wrong with you. A holiday to Bora Bora and then the Maldives, the Grand Canyon, maybe skydive? I've put it on there, but I think I would be too scared when it came down to it. Oh, and to have a small part in a movie! Granted, that might never happen, but it's on there anyway and loads more."

This girl was something else. She had ambition, and I liked that.

"I have kissed a dolphin, does that count?"

"Shut up! You've kissed a dolphin? Was she hot?"

We both burst out laughing. Luckily for me, I had just swallowed the remainder of my hot chocolate before the outburst.

"Yes, honestly. I was that lucky child that went to a waterpark on holiday and got to have a photo with a dolphin and kiss its nose. I can barely remember it if I'm honest. I was only about nine, but I'd love to swim with them, though."

"As if! I am so unbelievably jealous. I went on a cruise with my family around the Mediterranean, and the Captain would shout to the passengers every time there was a family of dolphins swimming past the boat. I was always the first one to nearly fall overboard, trying to look at them."

Her face lit up as she reminisced.

"They are amazing. So, the small part in a movie? What kind of movie are we talking about here? There are certain movies that you would certainly get cast in, but I didn't take you as that kind of girl."

I laughed as she playfully picked up a marshmallow from the side of her cup and threw it towards my face.

"You are bad. I am not that type of girl. I don't know. I just watch films all the time, and I think about how much I would love to be an actress. Like, to play a different person whenever you feel like it! I wonder if it feels like you are living more than one life, know what I mean? And they always look so glamorous and, not to mention; the women can't even act in most of the films that I watch. I feel like I would do a better job."

"Okay, so, working in a law firm isn't exactly what you aspire to do. Me neither, to be honest. I always wanted to start my own newspaper or magazine. I can see it now - a skyscraper in the middle of New York with an enormous, spinning sign that says, 'Holly's Times' or 'Garland Times' that has a nicer ring to it. What do you think?"

"I think the chances of that happening are about as slim as me winning an Oscar for Best Actress. I do admire your imagination, though; it's a very cool idea. How amazing would it be to publish everything you wanted in your own paper? I would cut the football out of the back pages straight away. No, thank you. I could add in a nice section about make-up or the week's fashion haves and have not's."

"Wow, okay. So, you like that idea. It would be very cool. Do you like to read?"

"Magazines? Or Books?"

"Either."

I was just intrigued to find out as much as I possibly could about Brooke. She fascinated me.

"Magazines, not so much. I buy the odd beauty magazine, but I'm not that interested when it comes to celebrity gossip. I like to read books, but I'm not the best reader. It does take me a good few months to get through a book, but I enjoy them. What about you?"

"No, to magazines, yes to books, although not as frequently as I would like. I work a lot of hours, and I'm usually seeing friends when I'm not working. It's difficult sometimes to fit in any sort of hobbies. I find something peaceful in going to the library, though. There's one not far from here, and it's so old fashioned, like what a real library should look like. I go there sometimes with my laptop. Not to do much, just surf the internet; it's peaceful. It's a great place just to sit and do nothing. If you have something on your mind or you're trying to figure something out, I would recommend it."

I soon realised that I had just rambled on. The last thing I wanted to do was bore Brooke, so I quickly stopped talking and waited for her reply.

"Why did you stop?"

"I had finished talking."

I was confused.

"Oh, well, I was waiting to hear more about this library; I'm intrigued."

She leaned against the table with one hand, propping her head up and urging me to continue talking.

I suddenly felt shy. I wasn't usually a shy person - I could stand in front of hundreds of people and give a speech, no bother. But then, in that moment, sat across from Brooke; I didn't know what to say. She found the most boring things I was saying interesting, things I always thought that nobody else would ever want to hear, and she wanted to hear more.

I spoke for the next twenty minutes about places I wanted to go, things I wanted to do, what I thought about the world today and an in-depth discussion about robots. It was a very odd conversation to have, and Brooke had her input on several topics but never said more than a few lines before urging me to carry on with my own opinion. It was as though she was fascinated with the way I spoke.

Imagine, all your life, hearing one accent or one particular voice and then, all of a sudden, hearing another. You would want them to keep talking, and that is the feeling I got from her: She wanted me to keep talking. I could tell by the way she held her head in her hand and moved her eyes with the rhythm of my lips. I felt obliged to continue.

It had been an hour since we entered the coffee shop and the manager changed the sign on the door to 'CLOSED' before kindly asking us if we could finish up our drinks (which we had done thirty minutes ago).

I knew we both needed to head home, but I had an overwhelming urge to find somewhere else, another coffee shop, a restaurant, anything at all, just so that I could keep talking to her. I didn't know whether to suggest it, but she spoke first before I opened my mouth.

"I had a nice time in there, Holly. I bet you can't wait to get home now. It's so cold out here. My dad said he would pick me up in the next ten minutes, so I don't have to get the train. I can wait here for him."

"Okay, no problem. Do you want me to wait with you until he comes?"

I was hoping she would say yes.

"Don't be silly! If we both stand here and freeze to death, who will work on all those cases? Hurry, go catch your train."

"Okay, but only if you're sure?"

One last chance for her to say yes, my heart sank.

"Holly, go away!"

She laughed and pushed me in the opposite direction.

"Goodbye, Brooke. Let me know when you're home safe, please, just so I know you aren't still here, stuck to the floor."

"Ditto. Goodbye, Holly."

I walked the length of the road until it got to the point where I had to turn towards the station. I looked back one last time, but she wasn't looking. I don't know if I'd expected a re-enactment of a scene from a movie, that standard look-back scene were both stars catch each other taking a second glance, hoping the other wouldn't notice. I had seen it a thousand times, but that wasn't the case then.

I don't know what I was thinking. She would never have been interested in me, even if I did happen to be single. I told myself that I needed to stop thriving off the first spot of attention I received, just because it had been something I was very unaccustomed to of late.

CHAPTER SIX

"What do you mean, you just went for coffee? Didn't you think to tell me you had finished work early? Or didn't I cross your mind at all?"

That was the situation I found myself in when I had returned home to Danielle. I was going to tell her I had been for coffee. I never kept things from her like that, even if it was something she might not have agreed with.

I had only been in the house for ten minutes when she came upstairs and perched herself on the edge of the bed. It wasn't until I received a text from Brooke, telling me that she was home with all fingers and toes frostbite free, that Danielle questioned precisely what I had been doing with my day.

"I'm sorry, Dan. It was a spur of the moment thing. The weather was awful, we both fancied a hot drink and we didn't want to wait out in the cold, that's all. I know I should have text you to tell you I'd finished work but, to be honest, I thought you would have been at work, and I know you can't reply half of the time."

I was hoping she would at least understand where I was coming from so I didn't have to continue the argument all evening.

"Yeah, that all seems fine to you, Holly, because you don't think about anyone but yourself. Imagine if this was the other way around. It wouldn't bother you in the slightest if I did that, would it not? Honestly?"

The worst thing I could've done at that moment was hesitate. I knew what she wanted to hear, and I could sense how vital it was for her to know I still cared as much as I used to. The truth always prevailed in the end and, the fact was, I didn't. It was a realisation that became clearer to me as the days passed by. The one thing I didn't want to happen was for it to become clear to Danielle. As the pain etched across her face, I could see I had failed.

"Save it, Holly. It's quite clear how you feel. If what I do doesn't bother you anymore, then I will do exactly what I want from now on."

As bad as I felt, I didn't have the energy to pursue her anymore. It became apparent that I was physically and mentally drained. When you fight with someone and try to make a relationship work for such a long period of time, it changes you. You really start to question everything you used to be - why is it so different? What went wrong? Could it have been prevented somehow?

If anyone can pinpoint just one solid answer for each of those questions, and say it with confidence, then you're fortunate. It all becomes a blur, a blur you no longer know how to control or how to fix.

My granddad used to say that you have to work at love. Love fades, and that's where people go wrong because they believe they need to find that again; the excitement, the butterflies and the overwhelming urge to go anywhere and do anything with that person. You get swept up in it but, years later, you find yourself bickering, disagreeing on 99% of things, arguing over who will pay the bill when you used to be so willing to pay for everything.

'That is life,' he used to say, *'But what you must understand is that the best relationships are the ones you fight for, the ones you never give up on, even when you can't see any other solution. If you give up, you will find someone else; you will fall in love again. It's inevitable. Years down the line, you will no longer be in love with that person, and you will be right back to the place you once thought was the end with someone else.'*

My grandma and granddad were married for 58 years. They met when they were both 16 years of age, but everyone knows it was a different generation back then, and unfortunately, the one thing we never took from that generation was how to make a relationship work. That's what scared me the most, giving up, losing something that, later in life, I would realise was so precious. How do you know if you are no longer in love or if you are just not right for each other? How do you decipher such a message? You can only go with your gut feeling.

My gut feeling was a mixture of many, and I had to decide what was best for everyone involved. I felt that my time was running out to do precisely that.

"What did I do to make you stop loving me?"

Ten minutes after the whole ordeal, I found myself stood in the doorway of my bedroom with my eyes transfixed on the crushed girl who sat before me. Tears filled my eyes, and I watched as hers became uncontrollable.

The sorrow that filled the room became so prominent. As unsure as I may have been about my relationship, then wasn't the time to voice the truth. I wasn't about to give up so quickly; I owed that to her.

"I never stopped loving you. I still love you."

It was true; I did still love her. Some lies would undoubtedly have to be told to spare her feelings, but that was not one of them.

"I see the tears in your eyes, Holly. I hear the sincerity in your voice, just as I always have. As heart-breaking as it is for me to admit, I no longer believe your words."

"Why would you question anything I tell you? Just because we haven't been perfect lately? Relationships are never easy, Danielle, but do not believe, even now, when things are difficult, that I do not love you. We can work through this rough patch, just like we have done before."

The tears running down her face subsided slightly as she spoke such resounding words.

"You will always want the very best for me; I know that. I also know you will stay with me for years to come, out of pity rather than love, because that's the kind of person you are. You would never intentionally want to harm me, and I know the sight of me crying upsets you deeply. I also know that I would be completely broken without you. I planned my future and saw no one else in it but you. You are the one for me, Holly. I believe that with all my heart, but am I the one for you?"

It seemed as though she was asking me the question, but she continued her outpour without giving me time to respond. I could only assume that she knew the answer.

"As much as I have hoped for all these years, the conclusion I come to says otherwise. Stand there now and tell me you want to spend the rest of your life with me. Tell me you cannot imagine a day when I am not yours, and maybe, just maybe, I will believe you."

Danielle flung her legs off the edge of the bed and sat with her head buried deep into her hands, waiting, dreading the response I would give.

"I do love you, Dan."

She sighed as the tears ran down her face.

"Then why do I feel so alone? The passion and the fire you had inside of you was so attractive to me. You made me feel like nobody came above me. I loved that, and I've craved that for so long now, to feel that again, to feel like your everything."

I could understand exactly why she felt that way. In the months leading up to that conversation, I had done nothing but work, see friends, see family. Come to think of it; I guess I had done almost anything to avoid seeing her. The whole conversation that evening had been a long time coming. It had stemmed from something so little but, to Danielle, it was so much more significant.

One thing I had done for a while, up until that point, was tell her exactly what she wanted to hear. It was a downfall of mine. I guess you could say I enjoyed the easy life. She gave me an easy life, 99 percent of the time. I guess you could say that was her downfall. It was also the reason that the situation had been brewing for a long time and never quite boiled over.

I couldn't help but feel, in that moment, that maybe it was time to do the right thing, not just for me and not just for her, but for both of us.

"I don't think I can be that person for you anymore, Dan."

I said it so quietly, almost muttering it under my breath as my heart sank completely. Telling the truth really did hurt sometimes.

"What do you mean? What are you saying?"

I didn't know what to say. I hadn't pre-empted the situation before I got home that afternoon. I had no time to prepare a speech, no time to plan what to say or, more importantly, how to say it. The whole thing had taken me entirely by surprise. I could do nothing other than tell her exactly how I felt.

"Holly, please, what do you mean? Is that it?"

She was desperate now, the silence making her pleas even more heart-breaking.

"The truth is, Dan, I don't know if we are right for each other anymore. I don't think I will ever be the person you want me to be, and I don't know if we will ever want the same things. A long time ago, yes, but now? I struggle to see our future."

There are certain things I find everyone says under those circumstances. It's almost like everyone reads from the same script when it comes to ending a relationship. Surprisingly enough, it becomes so natural at that moment in time.

She started to cry again, so completely lost for words that it made me break into tears as well. I tried to wipe the tears from her face as I sat down beside her on the edge of the bed. All I could do was hold her in my arms, my first and only instinct being to comfort her.

"I'm so sorry. Just believe me when I say that I never wanted it to turn out this way. I still love you; I have always loved you. Please don't ever doubt that."

Still no response.

"Danielle, please say something."

She pushed me away and stood up to head towards the door.

"I want you out. I won't keep you here any longer. If this is what you want, then you can leave, Holly. Just know that the grass isn't always greener on the other side. I gave you everything, all of me, and I would have done for the rest of my life. You go out there and find someone who loves you the way that I do. You won't."

She grabbed a bag from beside the door, quickly stuffed in some clothes from her wardrobe, went to the bathroom to gather her make-up and came back for her phone.

"Where are you going?"

"Don't act like you care, Holly. I'll be gone for a few days. I need time to clear my head, and it gives you time to get your things together. Don't call or text; I don't need your pity. You have made your decision."

Just like that, she was gone and out the door.

CHAPTER SEVEN

I lay on the bed that Danielle and I once shared, staring at the blank ceiling above and hoping the pang of guilt would soon disappear. It was just after 6 pm on the 17th of November and I hadn't spoken to Danielle for almost two days. I knew, deep down, that leaving her alone was the best thing to do. She needed some space, but at the same time, I didn't want her to think that I didn't care.

My phone had been relatively quiet all day. The occasional text from Paula or my mum was all that seemed to grace the screen. In the space of a few minutes, I could hear the loud ping of a text message occur, not just once but three times. I made my way downstairs to retrieve it from my work bag, expecting it to be about some complications regarding a case.

My heart sank when I saw the names on the screen.   I instantly felt guilty when I saw Danielle's name and then instant excitement when I saw Brooke's name above. I figured Brooke's would be the easiest to reply to and the least upsetting, so I opened that up first, intrigued to find out what it said.

Hi, Holly. Is everything okay? I don't want to pry. You've just seemed quiet and not yourself these past few days. I want to make sure you're okay and if you don't want to talk, that's fine, but I'm here if you need to.

I had barely spoken a word that wasn't completely necessary since Danielle left. Several people had asked me if I was okay. You don't realise how much people pick up on things; people you work with all day, every day, are going to notice when you aren't quite yourself. Most days, I went out of my way to have a friendly chat with Brooke, so she would undoubtedly know something wasn't right. I felt the need to put her mind at ease. I didn't want her to think it was anything she had done.

I'm okay, thank you for asking. I just have some stuff going on at the minute. Not quite sure I am ready to discuss it, but I appreciate you checking up on me.

Short and sweet. I guess you could say it was rather impersonal, but to be honest, I didn't know where Brooke and I sat on the scale of friendly to overly friendly. The fact I was even texting her, and she felt like she could ask if I was okay, was the trigger. That was something I swiftly put to the back of my mind when I remembered the second text message I had received—the one I truly dreaded.

I have told myself since I left not to send you the 'begging' message, the one that pleads for you to try again, for us to at least give it one more chance. There are a million things I wanted to say to you. I can't breathe thinking about my life without you. I see no other future or path I would take that doesn't have you in it. That's what is breaking me completely.
You are the one person I depended on, the one person I thought would always be there for me. I believed you when you

said forever - how foolish of me. I know I haven't exactly been easy to live with, so maybe it's my fault. I would've spent the rest of my life making you happy.

I don't know how you can just walk away from everything we have built together, eight years of memories as if it was nothing to you. How can you do that? A part of me hopes that you realise I am what you need and you won't give up on us. That's the only bit of hope I'm clinging to. I keep forcing myself to sleep, hoping I will wake up and it's all been a horrific nightmare.

I love you, and I hope you find it in yourself to remember how much you once loved me and maybe even still do.

Tears formed in the corners of my eyes and spilt onto the soft surface of my cheeks below. What on earth was my reply supposed to be to a message like that?

I had contemplated the idea of trying again so many times. I had even written a message asking her to come home countless times, but I knew better in the back of my mind.

This was the hardest part. Ending a relationship is easy; forcing yourself to move on and not go back becomes the hard part. I knew it was the right thing to do. I had finally concluded that I was doing the best thing for both of us but making her see it from my point of view was something entirely different.

I composed what I thought was a sincerely truthful reply.

I hate knowing how much you are hurting, how much pain I am causing you. This isn't as easy for me as you seem to think.

I have thought about you every second of every day, and I have replayed so many happy memories in my head. So many times, we have fought and tried again to keep alive what we once were. It has got to the point where one of us needs to be strong enough to realise it isn't working anymore.

I love you, that won't change tomorrow or the next day. I meant every word I ever said; sometimes, things just don't work out the way you plan. I know you probably hate me right now. I know I can't say anything that will make this any easier for you; I just hope you can forgive me one day.

That turned out to be one of many replies over the coming days. The messages got worse, and she pleaded until the pleading turned to anger, then the anger turned to spite and the circle repeated itself.

Danielle's mother dropped by to collect some of her things. She had decided to stay with her family until she felt strong enough to be on her own and, when that time came, she would choose to live elsewhere.

Living in the house where we had shared our life together was too difficult for her, and I completely understood why. It was almost eerie to wander around and have memories triggered from virtually every corner of the house. It felt empty. A photo frame reminding me of our first concert, another of our first holiday, even the grey lampshade in the corner and how we argued about it being the wrong shade and that it didn't quite match the curtains. I liked it, but of course, Danielle got her own way and the lampshade was exchanged.

There was a story behind almost everything. I tried not to dwell too much on what once was; I had to keep making steps forward; it was the only way.

The following weeks became one giant blur. I did nothing but work and sleep. Work was beyond busy, to the point where I did 12-hour days and only just managed a quick, half-hour lunch. I didn't mind it at the time; it took my mind off of everything else.

The big build-up to Christmas had started, along with everything that came with it. I was as unprepared as I ever was for the festive season. I would tell myself every year, 'I will be prepared' or 'I'll start buying in September and be wrapped in October'. It never happened and that year was no different. I told myself that it was because of my busy schedule and, usually, that would have been accurate but thinking about presents and Christmas trees only meant I had to come to the realisation that I was doing it all by myself.

It was the first Saturday of December and historically one of the busiest days of the year in London, particularly Oxford Street, but don't ask me why. I assume it had something to do with half of the country getting paid that week.

It was just over three weeks until Christmas, the season to be jolly, the time to be happy and spread the joy. I wasn't feeling too cheery, but the break-up was a decision I didn't regret.

The only thing that kept me sane at work was the thought of seeing Brooke. I had spoken to her most nights for almost two weeks. The conversation flowed so naturally and, before we knew it, it was 2 am and we were no closer to sleep. There was no intention of being more than friends, which I found incredibly odd. When she split up from Luke, I had been there for her, guided her through, giving her advice as any good friend would. At that stage, I didn't feel like I had any ulterior motives; I just wanted the best for her. It was clear that it wasn't him, and she found the long-overdue courage to accept that.

If I'm honest, I would never previously have spoken to a girl for that amount of time without it meaning something more. She was fast becoming a close friend and, the more I told her, the more I wanted to tell her. It was a bizarre feeling. I found myself checking my phone all the time. It didn't matter what I was doing; if I didn't have a reply from Brooke within 10 minutes, I was starting to question why. It was getting to a point where I couldn't wait to get home so I could sit in front of the TV all night and talk to her. I forgot to eat. I forgot to sleep. I forgot how to lead a normal life, all because of Brooke.

I continued to tell myself how odd the situation was. I knew we were just talking as friends but, in the back of my mind, I questioned whether it would always be as friends. I questioned why I wanted to talk to her as in-depth as I did and why she felt the need to confide in me the way she did.

There was something so angelic about the way she spoke as if she were the happiest girl alive. There was a sense of naivety about her, something I found myself wanting to protect the more I got to learn about her.

Brooke was a diamond in the rough in the sense that she was just a shy, ordinary girl. That wasn't a bad thing: She had the potential to be whoever she wanted to be, the sort of girl that minded her own business. She liked to be low key and, in her eyes, that was the best way. That was one of the many things I really liked about her.

That morning at work had been such a mad rush, and it was early afternoon before I had the chance to sit back and think about re-fuelling my body with something other than coffee. I had another five calls to return and at least ten emails to reply to. They would, no doubt, continue to build all day, so it was almost pointless to rush when working my way through them.

Brooke appeared in the doorway.

"What do you think about the research on the Williamson case? Have you had a chance to look?"

I flicked through the paper on my desk and pulled out the piece in question.

"I managed to have a glance earlier. Excellent work, Brooke. I think this one will be easier than I anticipated. I will go over it again later and let you know if anything is missing."

I could see the tired eyes and the exhaustion on Brooke's face. She had worked hard over the previous two weeks, and I wanted her to know that I appreciated it. A small smile of satisfaction crept upon her face.

"Some of the people in question didn't want to discuss what happened; others were a little more forthcoming, as you would imagine. I just think I'd like to try and get the daughter, Rebecca, on the phone again to clarify one or two things."

"I think you might be right. At first glance, her answers to things seem a little woolly. Maybe you'd be able to get more from her if you spoke again."

"I agree. Have a look through it properly, and just send me over any questions you'd like me to ask or anything you want me to clarify. I want it to be as solid as it can be, so I don't mind going back and digging a little deeper."

"Of course, I'll get around to it as soon as I can. Thanks, Brooke."

She smiled and nodded before swiftly leaving. I composed an email shortly after that I would send to all of my colleagues. Mr West wasn't one to organise big Christmas parties as he preferred to give a Christmas bonus which was better received by everyone. However, ever since I had been with the company, I had taken it upon myself to organise something. Even if it was a simple trip to the pub, I felt it was nice to take some time away to get to know my peers on a different level.

The email consisted of a few lines and an RSVP.

Hi All,

It's that time again! It's our annual team trip! I managed to pull a few strings and get a very small pot of 'loose change' from Mr Wes, so this weekend we are all going ice skating and then onto the pub afterwards for a few drinks if you fancy it?

Let me know as soon as possible so that I can arrange the numbers.
Hope to see you all there!

Holly

I knew most of them would be happy to go ice skating; it was different, and it was fun. I also knew that, for some, any form of physical activity would be frowned upon. I also knew those people would be persuaded more so by the trip to the pub afterwards.

All in all, I expected a rather positive reaction.

I had numerous replies over the coming hours, most really taking to the idea. Paula made it clear that she would need a metal frame to help her around the rink, but she was more than happy to try.

After reading through all the replies, it seemed like only one person had been ice skating recently and, therefore, had the upper hand on the rest of their colleagues. That person happened to be me.

My skills on the ice were absolutely nothing like they used to be. I had an uncle who used to play professional ice hockey when I was younger. He was more like a lifelong family friend that your mum insisted you call uncle, and he taught me a lot back then. I must have been on the ice every weekend for almost a year. I never continued after the age of thirteen, but I'd occasionally go, just to blow off the cobwebs.

I quickly ate the sandwich I'd made earlier that morning then it was time to get back to work. I was trying to get home at a reasonable time for once, determined to be sat in front of the television with the Chinese that I'd been thinking about all week.

I am ashamed to say I lived out of takeaway boxes once Danielle left. I could cook; that wasn't the issue. I had just become so lazy in the kitchen, and the last thing I wanted to do after a 12-hour day was to cook a pitiful dinner for one.

I got up to pour myself a cup of coffee before sitting back down at my desk. Almost immediately, my phone started ringing.

"Hi, sweetheart, it's your mum. Are you okay?"

It made me laugh every time my mother would call. I don't think she understood that caller ID was a thing, so she spoke as if I had no idea it was her calling.

"Hi, mum. Yes, I'm okay. Is it okay if I call you back later? I'm just a little busy at work, that's all."

"You're always busy at work. When are you going to take some time off?"

"Mum, it's Christmas. I'll be taking some time off soon, but I have a lot to do before then. You never ring at this time, is everything alright?"

"I just wanted to make sure you were okay; I haven't heard from you in almost a week. Also, Danielle's mum called me yesterday."

That took me by surprise. They were never close when me and Danielle were together, so why would she call her after we had split up?

"Oh, really? I didn't expect that. What did she have to say?"

"Nothing much, she was arranging how I would collect those bits I lent them for their holiday. She suggested giving them to you, but she didn't want to ring you and arrange anything. I don't think you're in her good books at the minute. She obviously held back her frustrations over the phone to me. It will be very one-sided on her part, though, won't it? She will see Danielle hurt and just assume you are the bad one in all of this, but I know that's not the case."

Of course, I was the bad person; I could've predicted that.

"Did you ask about Danielle? I haven't spoken to her in over a week, but I assume she's doing better because the late-night text messages have stopped."

"I didn't want to pry too much, as you can imagine. I just said that I hope she's doing okay, and it's a real shame that things didn't work out between you two because she is a lovely girl. You know I will always have your best interests at heart and, if she's not right for you, then only you know that. But she was a good girl and I hope, for her sake, she finds someone nice and I hope that you find someone who will love you the way that Danielle did."

"I know, Mum; I don't doubt that. When you know that something isn't right, you just know. It's difficult to explain, I guess. I need to go now, though. Enjoy the rest of your day. I'll speak to you soon."

"Okay, sweetheart. I'm here if you need me. I love you. Bye."

"I love you too."

It was pretty clear that going through a break-up was draining. There would always be a constant reminder of the other person, and people would always ask if you were okay. The reminders would continue for months after and, if it was hard for me, I didn't doubt that it would be harder for Danielle. I felt for her; I really did.

I managed to escape work shortly after 6 pm. It was a Thursday, exactly three weeks before Christmas, and I had the next two days off work. I didn't have much planned, just some well-deserved rest and the last few bits of Christmas shopping, maybe even a lunch date with a few friends.

I often had the same routine when leaving work on an evening. I would go to the local Starbucks for a latte or a hot chocolate on my way home. With the weather being as cold as it had been lately, the hot liquid made standing and waiting for the train or the bus that much easier.

There was one part of my routine that I changed slightly that evening. Instead of going to the Starbucks around the corner from work, I walked on another five minutes to a little, family-run coffee shop that sat on the corner. They had the most unique shop; a mixture of shabby chic, modern décor but with old fashioned church benches and beams as thick as the pavement outside. It was wonderfully put together, and the owner clearly had an eye for interior design.

There was a warmth to the shop as you walked in with candles upon every shelf and even more spread out across the tables. It had so much light, but in such an intimate way. It gave the whole room a romantic feel; you could imagine it being the perfect place to have a first date.

They didn't just serve coffee; they also served some of the best homemade cakes in the area. It made me wonder why I didn't go there more often, given that it was only five minutes away.

I had a taste for that particular coffee that day. I gained momentum going towards the corner of the coffee shop, constantly blowing my hands. My fingertips were cursing me for rushing and forgetting my gloves that morning. I felt the warmth explode through the coffee shop door as I turned the corner. A petite blonde head popped out, trying to hold a coffee, a cake and put her purse away, but it seemed she was struggling. The way she juggled all three was rather amusing and also familiar. It didn't take long for the store's lights to shine across her face, revealing her identity.

CHAPTER EIGHT

It took me a few seconds to break the silence. There was a moment between the two of us, which I couldn't explain, and it took me by surprise. I had to compose myself, and I quickly realised where I was and who I was stood with.

She looked different somehow, or maybe my eyes saw her differently. Her appearance was the same as it had been earlier that day, and yet she looked different.

"Brooke, here, let me grab that; you look like you're struggling."

"Thanks, Holly. I was scared I might miss my bus, but it seems they are all delayed today. Why can't they just run on time?"

"I wish I had an explanation for you. I have the same conversation with myself daily."

"With yourself, you say?" She laughed.

"In my head, of course. People might think I'm strange otherwise."

"More than they already do?"

The grin that followed was very flirtatious.

"Okay, cheeky. I'll have you know; I'm quite the catch. Strange or not strange."

I lowered my head to one side, focused my eyes and pursed my lips, a half-grin creeping across my face. I was waiting for her reaction, but I didn't think I would get the response I so desperately wanted until I saw her eyes.

They changed ever so slightly, only just enough that if I hadn't been staring right at them, I would have missed it. I was looking at her so intently without realising that I was probably making her feel uncomfortable. Instead of looking away, her eyes reflected my own; there was all of a sudden, a kind of understanding, a mutual agreement. She saw it too; she saw the change in my behaviour, and she reciprocated.

"I wouldn't disagree with that."

There was a nervousness between us now. It was unchartered waters we found ourselves in. She broke the gaze when she saw her bus arriving.

"There it is, I better get going. You go the opposite way, right?"

"Yes, I'll probably be waiting another 3 hours for mine, knowing my luck. Safe journey home, Brooke."

"Hopefully not. You should text me when you're home safe… if you want to, that is… Bye."

She jumped on the bus and kept her head down. The embarrassment was evident. What she said wasn't something you would say to a 'friend'; the intent behind the words seemed different somehow.

When I eventually arrived home, it was close to 8 pm. I was freezing, starving and ready for the comfort of my bed. Despite all this, the only thing that seemed to occupy my brain was the thought of talking to Brooke.

I thought about what I should do and what I wanted to do, two completely different things with two completely different outcomes. I felt like I was 16 again, back in the times when the only thing that mattered was speaking to your crush. I didn't want to seem too eager - just because she told me I should text her didn't mean that I had to. Don't get me wrong, I wanted too, but something in the back of my mind told me it was a bad idea. I fought the urge for an hour before I eventually fell to sleep.

It was the weekend of our team bonding trip/Christmas get-together. My two days off work had gone incredibly quick. Once I had cleaned the house, my car, been shopping and done all the other menial chores, there was hardly any time for myself. The only plus was that it kept me busy. I told myself so many times I would do nothing on my day off, just sit in front of the TV and watch old films, but it never happened. Shortly after the first film began, my mind would wander onto what else I should be doing.

I hadn't spoken to Brooke since I'd seen her outside the coffee shop, although she had been firmly on my mind since that evening. I felt terrible for not texting her, but there was some reasoning for my madness. At least I told myself there was.

I had been out shopping for a new outfit. I didn't necessarily have anything in mind, but I had hugely exceeded my shopping budget that month, so I was looking for something on the cheap. I was never really good at cheap and, nearly £150 later, I had myself a new outfit.

I purchased some new brogues from Topshop. I was due a new pair which I would also wear for work (the only way I could justify the expense). The second purchase was an impulse buy. I had been telling myself for months that I needed a new pair of jeans, bearing in mind I already had enough pairs to open my own store. This pair was slightly different, though.

Again, that's what I told myself. I also needed some new perfume and some new earrings.

I still had clothes in my closet with tags on, unopened bottles of perfume, at least ten pairs of shoes that I had only worn once. I guess the moral of the story is: If you like it, buy it.

I nipped into the local shop on the way home to get myself a drink. I had been parched on the train ride back and, assuming I had all the time in the world; it hadn't occurred to me to check my phone. I had ignored it entirely until it began beeping excessively in my pocket.

It was a string of text messages from Paula.

I'm here.
I thought I would come early to make sure the booking was all okay.
What time will you be here?
I think a few of the girls have just turned up.

I looked at the time in the top right-hand corner: It was just after 6 pm. I had 30 minutes to get ready and get to the ice rink before the evening session started at 6:30 pm. I had planned to be there around the same time as Paula to make sure everything went smoothly. I quickly texted her back as I got home.

OMG, Paula, I don't know where my head has gone. I have just walked in. I'll get ready as quickly as I can. You guys get on the ice without me; I may be a bit late.

Paula would be rolling her eyes at the text. It wasn't the first time I had been late to something I had arranged myself. I had the quickest shower known to man, and getting ready commenced at 6:11 pm. I was ready by 6:34 pm. Luckily for me, my make-up was still intact from earlier in the day, and I was having a pretty good hair day for once.

The ice rink wasn't far from my house, so I ordered a taxi for 6:40 pm and arrived ten minutes later.

Everyone had already made their way onto the ice by the time I arrived. A few guys from the firm were a little more hesitant and trailed the edges of the rink, waiting for their opportunity to step on. It didn't take me long to get my skates on and, within minutes, I was gliding across the ice to get to Paula, who stood cautiously in the far corner.

The response was one I expected,

"Here she is, finally, Miss I'm-late-for-everything."

Her smirk gave away her pretend-disappointed face.

"Hey, that's not true! There was that one time… when we went to… Okay, you got me, I am terrible. You are the Queen of everything and amazing at being on time. I am truly sorry."

"Well, yes, I am the Queen but, to be fair, you're not often late for work, so I'll let you off. Just being on time for social events isn't your strong suit. God, you must be awful to date, keeping those women waiting around all the time."

I laughed out loud dramatically.

"Who are all these women because I would love to meet them?"

She laughed, almost fell over and then quickly regained her balance. It was a comical sight.

"Whose idea was this, seriously? I think the last time I went ice skating; dinosaurs were around. I have no balance, and it's freezing. Who knew the ice would be so cold? FYI, if I fall and break a hip, I'm suing you."

I barely heard a word she was saying over the sheer laughter erupting from my mouth. She often had rants like this and they were, more often than not, very comical. The more she ranted, the less steady her balance became. I couldn't breathe; it was the most I had laughed in a very long time. Eventually, I gave her a helping hand to steady her feet, once I'd composed myself, of course.

"Are you done?" I managed to squeeze out through fits of laughter.

"Oh, piss off, you. If I could actually skate on my own without your aide, I'd be leaving you behind."

"Yes, but, unfortunately, you can't. I think Bambi would do a better job."

The laughter continued as we threw insults back and forth. That is what I loved about Paula, never a dull moment.

"I am already in need of a drink, and guess what, you're buying."

"I totally agree. First-round is on me after that comedy show."

There was a moment's silence before the conversation took a turn.

"On a serious note, Holly. When will you be back on the market?"

I thought it was a rather strange question but chose to make light of it, as always.

"Well, Paula, I didn't realise you liked me that way; I could've sworn I wasn't your type. I'm missing the beard and something between my legs that I was told you rather enjoyed."

She hit me before continuing, nearly falling over yet again.

"Seriously, you idiot. I may have a proposition for you, and it doesn't involve me before you start."

My ears soon pricked up and I was intrigued.

"Honest answer, I am 100% back on the market. I'm not looking for anything serious, though. I know that's what everyone says, but I was with Danielle for a long time. I'm not ready to settle down again, and I don't think I will be for a long time."

I half-believed the words I was saying, but I knew, deep down, it wasn't as easy as that.

"That's what I wanted to hear. Do you remember me telling you about my friend, Lisa? Well, her best friend is a lesbian. She's a lot younger than us, so I'm not trying to set you up with some cougar before you ask. She's stunning, and she said she found you really attractive – I think it was that photo I posted of us on Facebook a few months back."

"What's her name? Do I know her?"

"I'm not sure if you know of her or not, but she's called Olivia Darton."

The name didn't ring any bells.

"Nope, I don't think I do. I may have to check her out. I think it's time I got myself back out there."

"I totally agree! She's lovely and just your type. I've met her once or twice, and she seems sweet. I'm sure she will be out next weekend for Lisa's birthday. Why don't you come?"

"That's a very tempting offer. I'll get back to you."

I don't know why I said that; it wasn't like I had plans or someone whose permission I needed to ask. I never liked to agree to things straight away. There was something about committing to a time and a place that I struggled with. Clearly, I wasn't very good at being on time anyway, so maybe that had something to do with it.

"Suit yourself. More fool you if you don't come. Anyway, I'm just about getting the hang of this, so I'll let you mingle, seeing as you planned this whole team bonding session. Adios."

She held on to the side of the rink like it was a pot of gold, not letting go. It was safe to assume that I would be picking her up off the floor at some point that evening.

I made my way around the ice, dodging one child after another as they flew past. I was once that age, thinking I was invincible until I fell and cracked my chin wide open. I was the child that had to be escorted off the ice by paramedics.

I felt underneath my chin. It was still there, the small indent left from the set of stitches I'd needed.

I looked around me. It was jam-packed; there was 15 of us in total that night, a good turnout. It was so busy that I could barely make people out. In the far corner, I saw Paula skating with two of the older, more established lawyers on the team. To the right, I saw James and Ryan, both accompanied by their girlfriends. Then there was Lacy, Cara and Harriett being chatted up by a group of men.

As I continued to skate around, my eyes met the one person's I was looking for, but she looked away instantly. I wondered how long Brooke had been looking my way, given I had been there almost 45 minutes and hadn't seen her once. I felt she was avoiding me because she would typically make eye contact and smile, maybe even wave, but she couldn't look away quickly enough. I found that rather strange.

She was stood with her friends, which made me hesitant to approach her, but I had no real reason to feel uncomfortable. To everyone else, she was just a work colleague. Regardless, I skated over and imposed myself casually on their conversation.

"Hi, guys. We enjoying the ice?"

A chorus of 'hello's' mumbled back before one of the girls answered for the group.

"I'm really enjoying myself. A few of us nearly fell over in the first ten minutes, but I think we have got the hang of it now. Well, I don't know about Brooke; she's looking a little bit shaky."

They all looked over at Brooke and laughed. She was slightly embarrassed and her face flushed before she could compose herself and laugh along.

"Ice skating isn't a skill I possess, but I'm getting there."

Stacey gave her a reassuring pat on the shoulder before suggesting something.

"Why don't you have Holly teach you a few things? If you used to skate, you must be as good as any of these instructors, right, Holly?"

It was almost like the girls were forming a plan. Did they know something I didn't? I wasn't about to blow my own trumpet but teaching her wouldn't have been out of my comfort zone. I found it odd that Brooke hadn't made eye contact with me since I came over, and I was curious as to why. I needed to get her on her own for a few minutes so I could ask, and it seemed like the perfect opportunity.

"I am a little rusty, but I could show you the basics if you like, Brooke."

Her eyes shot towards her friends and then back at me with a smile on her face that was blatantly fake before responding.

"Sure, why not?"

"We will carry on skating around, find. Find a little bit?"

Brooke barely had a chance to nod and agree before her friends shot off, leaving a slight awkwardness in the air. It didn't take me long to break the silence.

"So, before we start, is it just me or are you being off with me?"

"Why would I be off with you?"

"I'm asking you that question. I feel the tension in the air, and it's not normally like that with us. I just want to make sure I haven't done anything to upset you in any way."

"Would it even bother you if you did?"

"Of course, it would. I wouldn't want to upset anyone that I work with or anyone at all, for that matter."

Okay, maybe it was a little low to treat her as if she was just someone I worked with; after all, we had grown closer as friends since my split from Danielle, but we didn't hang out together outside of work, and I only knew her through work, so what else was I supposed to categorise her as.

"Okay, I understand. You haven't upset me in any way, so don't worry about it. I'm just not feeling myself lately and I find it a little odd that you're talking to me as if we are friends when we clearly are not. Let's be fair; I work under you, don't I? I'm not a fancy lawyer, so technically, you're my senior. I don't know what I expected."

Matters were getting a little confusing at that point. I didn't want to make anything worse or cause a scene.

"Okay, if that's how you see it, then I'll let you get back to your friends. To be honest, this whole thing is confusing me."

"I agree. I'll see you later."

I had no idea what had just occurred. She was an absolute whirlwind. One minute she seemed annoyed and, the next, she skated away like nothing bothered her. I had an overwhelming urge to go after her. I enjoyed Brooke's company and something about that night wouldn't have been the same if she wasn't there to talk to. I was intrigued to know if she felt the same way. Suppose one tiny part of her wanted to spend time with me too. How on earth do you put that across to someone with who you are simply just friends?

Then it occurred to me.

You have a few drinks.

CHAPTER NINE

The drinks started flowing. I put £100 behind the bar for everyone to have a drink on me, it wouldn't go far, but I was feeling rather generous. It was nearly Christmas, after all. The Green Bar was a great place to be, only a 5-minute walk from the ice rink and the kind of atmosphere that instantly puts you in a good mood. The cocktails were always 2 for 1, which, of course, made it even more appealing.

As I walked through the door, there was a seating area to the right crowded with people trying to have a conversation above the music's blare. In the middle of the room lay a giant dance platform and pole, often used by the more inebriated ladies towards the end of the evening. Further on, more seating spread down the walls, all the way down to the bar at the back. The bar spanned the entire length of the club, displaying every alcohol you could imagine.

The Green Bar was well known for having the more exotic alcohols as well as the expensive kind, the likes of Remy Martin Champagne and Belvedere Vodka. It wasn't the most extensive bar; I would say 150 people would fit comfortably. The only lights in the bar were green (hence the name) which made for a different kind of atmosphere, a more relaxed one, even when the music picked up.

My poison for the evening was one my body had grown accustomed to, margaritas. It wasn't until my fourth that I began to assess the situation.

I had been watching Brooke since we got to the bar. She looked terrific; I couldn't help but admit that. All the women had taken a change of clothes and their make-up to the ice rink so that, after we had finished, we could prepare for the rest of the evening.

She had changed into a little shiny, black dress and a low cut one, at that. The dress complemented her in every way, showing off the figure that was usually hidden underneath her smarter work attire.

How did I broach the subject?

How did I bring it up without being too obvious about the fact I actually cared?

I knew that if I left it any longer, it would end up being the margarita talking which would undoubtedly end badly.

I made my way over to Brooke. The music was loud, leaving me with no choice but to whisper in her ear, making it even more intimate than I would've wanted. I had to get it right.

"Can I talk to you?"

Her eyes were ever so slightly glazed and, by the looks of it, she was ahead on the drinks.

"Sure, what about?"

I gently took her arm and led her over to the corner of the room, away from prying eyes. She didn't resist. In fact, her body seemed to welcome my touch as I led her away from her friends.

"Okay, do you think you could tell me why you were different with me earlier? Don't pretend you weren't. I have spoken to you quite a lot lately, Brooke. I can tell when you're not yourself."

"Holly, why are you obsessed with knowing if I'm okay or not? What does it even matter? I'll be completely honest with you; I wasn't myself, but not because of anything you've done. It's my own stupid fault for thinking something more of a situation which isn't what it seems."

I was taken aback by the tone in her voice, one I wasn't used to.

"What do you mean, 'it isn't what it seems'? The last time I saw you, outside the coffee shop, everything was fine between us. Now, there's tension, and I want to know why."

She rolled her eyes.

"Do I need to spell it out for you? I felt like an idiot, okay? A huge idiot because I asked you to text me, and you didn't. I don't know what I was thinking in the first place. As sad as it sounds, I spent the whole night waiting for you to text. I even considered texting you until I realised how ridiculous I was being. You have no interest in me and that's fair enough. I got my wires crossed."

I could see the instant regret on her face, realising that she had maybe said too much.

"I didn't think you had any interest in me?"

"Well, I didn't think that either. I don't know; it's complicated for me. I have never felt this way about a woman before. It's not the same feeling I get when I talk to my other friends. I always find myself wondering what you are doing. The only reason I came here tonight was to see you; otherwise, I probably wouldn't have bothered."

They do say that alcohol brings out the truth, but she hadn't admitted anything too critical. Basically, it bothered her when I didn't text her and it was a revelation to me, an insight into how she may be feeling. Maybe she looked at me in the way I looked at her. Perhaps she even thought about what it would be like to… I was getting way ahead of myself; it was time to reign it in.

"Are you saying you like me?"

"I'm not sure what I'm saying! I am so confused. All I know is that I want to talk to you all the time. I constantly fight the urge to send you a text."

"Do you want me to let you in on a secret?"

"As long as it's a good one."

"I enjoy talking to you. I sometimes fight the urge to text you too, like I did the other night after the coffee shop."

Her eyes lit up for a second. I knew she'd heard me; the music was so loud, but we both seemed to be getting the majority of the conversation through.

"Well, don't fight the urge in future. Just talk to me. What's wrong with that? If you enjoy talking to me, talk to me. Don't let me sit at home all night thinking there was something wrong with me, and that's why you didn't text me."

We both smiled. It seemed we had come to some mutual agreement. Although I wasn't quite sure what it was, it was certainly better than the atmosphere that had lingered earlier that night.

"Okay, so, for now, we both agree to text each other whenever we feel the urge?"

"That is exactly what we agree on. I expect at least 200 text messages a day, Holly."

She laughed, softly running her hand down the side of my neck before she turned to walk away; even that slight touch gave me a shiver.

The next day arrived with what could only be described as the worst hangover in the history of hangovers.

I would often forget the consequences that drinking had on my normal bodily functions. To put it as simply as I could, I felt like a train had hit me, followed by a bus and then a car. I missed being 18 and waking up with no aftermath of the obscene amount of alcohol I had consumed the night before.

What I would give to go back to that.

The rest of the evening had been a raving success, so I had been told. I didn't remember much after midnight, but I was told Brooke ordered me a taxi, proving herself to be the sensible one out of the two of us.

I promptly reviewed my texts, looking for evidence of any wrongdoing. I had sent messages to three people, telling them I had arrived home safely. It was more like a text from a five-year-old child, but the intention was there.

It wasn't until I opened the thread of text messages to Brooke that I realised just how much of a liability I had been.

The last three messages were almost unreadable. I had tried to tell her I was home safe, that I loved her company, and I wished I could kiss her. It had been sent over five messages with numerous spelling mistakes and several inappropriate emojis, and to top it off, she hadn't even replied. She had been so embarrassed for me that she didn't know what to say.

It was damage control time. I could've composed a long, apologetic message, but maybe it wouldn't be too bad if I played it cool.

Good morning, how is your head? I heard you helped me find my way home last night. I just wanted to say thank you. It turns out the older I get, the less responsible I become. Who would've thought it?

I knew It wouldn't take her long to reply; it never did. A minute later, I had a reply.

Well, good morning, heavy drinker. I think I sobered up after a few hours; I was too busy looking after my friends and you, for that matter. I'm not complaining, though. My head is magnificent, but after your eventful night, I'm going to take a wild guess and say that yours isn't?

I wondered what she found so eventful, other than my inability to control myself.

Well, that's good then. What was so eventful about the evening? Hopefully, it wasn't me making a fool of myself? My head is questionable.

The reply was instant.

YOU.

Extremely to the point but one word that lead to so many different questions.

Me? I'm not sure whether that's a good or a bad thing. Please elaborate.

I had either left an excellent impression or a horrible one, but she was still speaking to me, which left me with some hope.

Don't worry; it wasn't all bad. I found you very funny but the woman you spilt your drink on probably didn't. Please tell me you remember that?

Phew.

No? I am a disgrace. Other than the poor woman, I didn't do anything else, did I?

I lay in bed, praying to God that there was nothing else I needed to know. The usual 30-second reply stretched to two minutes and then five minutes as she continued to type and then retype, almost as if she was afraid to say something. The minutes felt like hours, but it always seemed to be that way when I waited for an important text.

You did do one other thing... Well, it was something you said, not did. After one too many tequilas, you told me you really wanted to kiss me. I don't believe it was anything other than alcohol-related, so don't worry.

So much for playing it cool; clearly, that had not been something I was very good at. The way I saw it, I had two options; I could make out it was all down to the alcohol or I could admit that maybe I had wanted to kiss her. She was already downplaying the comment, which made option one the easiest. I felt like a school kid.

Who knew that, at 28 years of age, I would still be sat in bed, extremely hungover, contemplating whether or not to tell a girl that I liked them. I had never been good at playing games. I wasn't one to beat around the bush or manipulate situations; I was straight to the point.

I had to work with Brooke, and that brought up several complications. I had to consider those potential complications before I opened myself up.

I quickly realised as I sat contemplating that over ten minutes had passed. I had no idea what to say, but I figured honesty was the best policy.

Oh, wow, I do apologise. It turns out I can be a bit of an idiot when I'm intoxicated.

Short and sweet.

Well, to be honest, you claimed you wanted to kiss me, but you did, in fact, make out with Sarah. I was rather shocked. I didn't realise she was your type or was that also alcohol-driven?

I did briefly recall kissing Sarah. We had a very good relationship, so I knew it wouldn't be made into anything more than what it was, but I could sense a hint of jealousy in Brooke's tone; she was fishing. I wasn't sure what for, so I decided to tell her exactly what I thought she wanted to hear.

My type? I don't have a type, but Sarah would certainly not be it. She's a good friend, so I'm sure she didn't mind too much haha. Yes, to the alcohol-driven. The majority of things I do tend to get me in trouble but, if that's all I did, I will take that as a win.

I couldn't lie in bed for much longer; I needed Paracetamol and some form of food to try and cure a small part of my awful hangover. My phone pinged again as I entered the kitchen.

You must have a type? My advice to you would be don't drink as much next time haha.

Okay, so I do have a type; I think everyone does. If you had to describe your dream man or woman, some characteristics would pop into your head straight away, whether it be blonde or brunette, blue eyes or green, height, weight, the list is endless. Although we may end up in a string of relationships with completely different people, when it comes down to it, there are specific characteristics we would choose. Right at that moment, I was thinking deeply about what I would look for, and several, if not most of the characteristics, pointed towards Brooke.

That surprised me and I slowly realised that she possessed so much of what I wanted or, at least, what I felt I needed.

It would be too much of a cliché to tell her that, to basically describe her in a message. Instead, I went with the opposite of Brooke and that's when the conversation came to a rapid halt. Her reply was short and precise.

I hope you find her.

CHAPTER TEN

It was Saturday 15th December, exactly ten days before the big day. The only day out of the whole year with a build-up of 12 months. The spirit of Christmas was undoubtedly everywhere I looked, from decorations to Christmas trees to carol singers.

There was a choir performing outside the West & Barnes building every day that week, and after the first day, I was already overcome with hatred for the songs. It wasn't the songs themselves but the incessant repetition. They played everywhere I went, not to mention being every other song on the radio, and it became a chore to indulge the whole song after a while.

Don't get me wrong; I love Christmas. I guess I just had certain tolerances, and carols were not one of them.

That afternoon at work was slow. I didn't often go into work on a Saturday, but I felt the need to get ahead of my caseload with the festivities rapidly approaching. The hands on the clock slowly ticked by; I glanced, every so often, at the doorway, hoping a certain someone would be in work that day. I knew that wasn't the case, but it didn't stop my constant distraction.

My head wasn't where it needed to be, so an easy day was all I had hoped for. I had done nothing but think about the way

Brooke had been with me the night before. It was strange; everything had been great, we spoke most nights and it had slowly crept into the day. I couldn't remember going more than a few hours without talking to her that past week. It seemed too good to be true, the way we connected. It was on a different level to anything I had experienced before, and for that reason, I was weary.

When you start to feel strongly towards someone, it's almost too much to control. My mind was working overtime; every thought I had went back to her. I could be anywhere with anyone, but I would constantly be checking my phone, awaiting her reply. My whole week revolved around waiting to speak to Brooke and that's when I knew something had switched. There was a sudden expectation in the air, which was the scary part: With expectation came problems.

I had seen her on Friday at work, and things had been normal up until halfway through the day when she went cold. I had approached her to ask about her plans for the evening and she shut me down, almost instantly, before walking away to carry on with her work. That wasn't like Brooke; she would always stop and talk; she would always engage in conversation. I wanted to go after her and make sure she was okay, but my presence had been requested in one of the meeting rooms; after that, I never found the time.

I did text her that evening, asking if she was okay, but I got no reply. I text her again the following morning but, again, no response.

After thinking about every possible thing that could've gone wrong, I was just as clueless as I had been earlier that day. I made a last-ditch attempt at trying to understand the situation by asking one of her closest friends. That might have seemed like a silly thing to do, but I was running out of options.

Bethany also worked at the law firm. They had both gone through university together and ended up with placements at the same law firm, much to their delight. I had never gone out of my way to speak to Bethany, but she seemed like a nice girl, and I knew they were close, so close that she would tell her about how much we had been talking, I hoped. I saw an opportunity.

"Bethany, how are you? Sorry to bother you but do you have a minute?"

She looked at me with a friendly face, although slightly confused.

"I'm great, thank you, Holly. How are you? Of course, I have a few minutes. What can I do for you?"

I could tell she was puzzled, so I got straight to the point.

"Great, thank you for asking. Can I ask you a question?"

She looked concerned but nodded.

"I know you're one of Brooke's closest friends, and I was just wondering if something is going on in her personal life. Is she okay? She seemed a little upset yesterday and I wanted to make sure everything was okay."

I think I came across as sincere, like I was genuinely concerned. Bethany hesitated for a second before answering.

"I spoke to her this morning and she seemed absolutely fine then. She would've told me if anything major was happening, so she was probably just tired or something. She can get a little moody when she's tired, but it's nice of you to show concern."

Before I had the chance to respond, she spoke again.

"She's finally agreed to go on a date tonight with a guy I've been trying to set her up with for weeks, so she must be fine. She seemed keen to go."

If it wasn't obvious to Bethany that my face had just dropped, then she wasn't as bright as I thought she was. I tried to hide the disappointment on my face, but I wasn't sure I was doing the best job.

"Oh, really? That's nice for her. Is he taking her somewhere nice?"

I tried to keep my voice as unaffected as I could. I shouldn't have felt that way, but my heart was in my stomach.

"Yeah, it will be good for her to let her hair down; she's seemed very pre-occupied lately. I think they're just going to the cinema, maybe a few drinks afterwards. Dates can take you anywhere these days, can't they."

She was genuinely thrilled for Brooke, and you could see it when she spoke.

"Well, good for her. Tell her I said I hope she has a lovely time, won't you? I will leave you to get on with your day; I can see you're busy."

I walked away with a horrible feeling in the pit of my stomach. I had gone over intending to find out what was wrong with Brooke, hoping it would be something bigger than me, something she would explain and apologise for in a few days so we could go back to normal.

I was completely and utterly deflated.

Why would she go on a date with someone? I guess what I thought was happening between us wasn't as mutual as I had hoped for. Maybe she'd decided she didn't want to continue talking the way we had been. Why couldn't she of just told me that, rather than ignore my text messages? I was frustrated and ready to go home with the hopes of forgetting the day's events.

It took all of 20 minutes for me to regret being sat in the house alone. I should've taken my friend up on his offer of going for a drink.

Jake was one of my closest friends and had been since school. I didn't see him as much as I would've liked due to our conflicting work schedules, but I knew he was always there. He worked nights as a security guard all over London, mainly in the Soho area, and he would often invite me for a drink on his occasional night off or before he was due to start a shift. I had said no because I was in a terrible mood that I found incredibly hard to shake. It was almost 8 pm, and I wasn't working in the morning, so I refused to sit there and mope.

I quickly grabbed my phone.

Jake, on second thoughts, I'll take you up on that offer. I could really do with a drink.

I threw my phone on the bed and quickly went to change. I already had on a nice denim shirt, black jeans and a black trench coat, so all I required was some warm boots. The weather had dropped to almost freezing the day before, so it was definitely time to pull out the winter necessities. I quickly brushed my teeth and fixed my hair in the mirror; three squirts of my newest Chanel fragrance and I was ready to go.

I was stepping out into the freezing cold no more than ten minutes after sending the text. I knew Jake would be starting work around 11 pm so I didn't have much time to get to Soho.

I was sat on a relatively quiet underground tube. I loved riding at night and, although it was still bustling, it was nothing compared to the hustle and bustle of the day. I was on the train for two minutes, give or take, when my phone beeped its usual text tone. I was in no rush to pull it from my jacket pocket as I assumed it would only be Jake checking how long I would be. It wasn't until I looked, a few minutes later, that I realised it wasn't Jake, it was Brooke.

My heart skipped a beat; the thudding in my chest prominent. I was nervous about opening the message, but I wasn't sure why. What's the worst that could happen? I asked myself. Maybe she'd tell me she had really hit it off with the mystery guy and she didn't want to talk to me anymore; I guess that would've been the worst. I know that I was overthinking things, given that we had never spoken about being anything more than friends. Yes, we flirted and we admitted that we enjoyed each other's company, but that's all. I toyed with the idea of opening the text for what felt like an eternity before I eventually plucked up the courage, it read.

I spoke to Bethany and she said you asked if I was okay. She also said your face looked like a picture when she told you I was going on a date? In answer to your question, yes, I am okay. Nothing that a few drinks and a distraction can't cure.

I was secretly hoping it would've got back to Brooke. If she knew that I knew she was going on a date, maybe she'd explain why. It seemed to have worked. I had to find out what was going on.

I can't lie; I couldn't hide my disappointment. Are you going to tell me why you have refused to text me back for the past two days?

I wasn't aware of her whereabouts, she very well could have still been on the date, but I wasn't beating around the bush. I wanted to know what I had done so wrong.

I'm kidding myself, that's why. I like you, but I'm obviously not right for you and that's why you're looking elsewhere. I have accepted that we are friends and friends don't talk the way we do, so I'm distancing myself from whatever this is.

Confusion set in. Why was she saying that? We were

friends, but we both knew that there was something more between us on some level.

What do you mean, I've been 'looking elsewhere'? I don't understand why you're saying these things if I'm honest. Please explain.

I stared at my phone, the tiny bubbles in the bottom left of the screen appearing then disappearing. I wondered what was going through her head, what she wanted to say but dare not write.

Eventually, the response came through.

Why didn't you just tell me you had a thing for Hannah? Everyone at work is talking about it. It seems I'm not the only person you like to talk to. It made me feel like just another silly girl, taken under your spell. I thought you would've told me something like that. We speak non-stop and you forget to mention that you're also talking to Hannah? Why did you keep that a secret from me, Holly?

There must have been a huge misunderstanding somewhere and now she thought I was talking to someone else.

Hannah Merloft was a fellow lawyer. She was a few years older than me. I wasn't the type to be overly confident when it came to women, but it was clear she liked me; I could tell that much. If anything, I tried my best to avoid her so I could, in turn, avoid rumours. It was apparent by Brooke's message that I had been unsuccessful, and the rumour mill had started.

Listen, I am not speaking to Hannah, nor have I ever been speaking to her in any other way than strictly professional. So, whoever told you that has heard something completely untrue

Now it was starting to make sense.

Why don't I believe you? Anyway, it's none of my business; it just made me re-think a few things.

I would love to have known who started the rumour about Hannah and me. It was up to Brooke whether or not she chose to believe me, but I was telling the truth and that's all I could do.

Well, I'm telling you that it's not true. I don't know why I am explaining myself to you. Like you said, it's none of your business. Besides, you can't talk after going on a date tonight.

Things were getting a little confrontational and that is not what I wanted. She was my friend, at least, I thought she was. I had confided things in her that nobody else knew. I regretted the message as soon as I'd sent it.

I can go on a date with whoever I please and so can you. You can do whatever you want, Holly. If the rumours aren't true, then you might want to talk with Hannah.

I didn't know how to respond. Whilst being so engrossed in my conversation with Brooke, I'd completely forgot to get off at my stop. I had no choice but to get off at Covent Garden and catch the next tube back to Tottenham Court.

I quickly text Jake, apologising for the delay, and I clicked back onto Brooke's text. How was I supposed to respond to that? I didn't want things to get sour between us, but I wasn't entirely sure how the conversation had played out the way it did in the first place.

My logic was simple: Anyone that just wanted to be friends wouldn't have reacted the way she had and, if all I wanted were to be friends, my heart wouldn't have sunk the way it did when I found out about her date.

There was something that neither of us wanted to admit.

I exited the train and waited behind the yellow line. It was eerie that night, and there was a dozen other people on the platform, all going about their day. I took the time to formulate a response quickly.

I will quash the rumours as soon as I can. I'm sorry if it upset you. Can we go back to normal now?

The last thing I wanted was to carry on falling out and potentially cause irreparable damage.

Did me going on a date upset you?

That was an easy question to answer.

Yes.

The bubbles appeared and disappeared several times. What was she thinking?

Good. I wanted to know how you felt; now I have my answer.

Was she testing me? She had gone on a date because she knew I would find out, and she wanted to gauge my reaction.

I'm glad I passed your test. How was the date? Did sparks fly?

Okay, so I was being slightly sarcastic but I was intrigued.

As a matter of fact, they did. He was my ideal date; funny, charming, generous, handsome, he ticked all the boxes. I'm actually on my way to his apartment now.

She had to be lying! If she was trying to make me jealous, it was working. Before I had time to respond, a second message came through.

Obviously, I'm joking. On a serious note, it was okay. If I am completely honest, I couldn't help but think about you.

That was like music to my ears; a grin took over my entire face. She actually thought about me; that had to mean something. I had this overwhelming urge to see her. I didn't want to wait anymore.

I want to see you.
Now.
Please.

I heard a beep, then another one; It sounded close by. I sent another text; I heard another beep. I looked to my left, then to my right, but I couldn't figure out where the sound was coming from, so I text again.

Where are you?
Are you in the un...

The last text sent before I had a chance to finish it; the beeps had grown closer. I looked to my left and there she stood, no more than 10 feet away.

She stepped onto the platform, unaware of my presence. She wore black boots with just enough heel to elongate her legs perfectly. She wore a fitted khaki dress that sat just below the knee, finished off with a leather jacket draped casually over her shoulders. Considering it was freezing out, she didn't look cold; she oozed style and sophistication.

A small gust of wind came through the tunnel as the train on the opposite side went by. The slight breeze was enough to send a shiver down my spine but for all the right reasons. The gust blew Brooke's long hair from her face, the way it does in the movies, and she looked incredible. I took every last bit of her in, and it wasn't until my jaw was about to hit the floor that she saw me.

We locked eyes.

I smiled; she smiled.

We just knew.

CHAPTER ELEVEN

There are moments in life that happen unexpectedly, without any forethought, almost on a complete whim. Those moments, I believe, are usually the best you will ever experience, the only downfall being that they happen so fast, leaving you wondering if it was all a dream.

12 hours earlier…

I pushed Brooke through the doors of the underground's toilets. She grabbed my neck in a passionate embrace, bringing my lips down to hers again and again. There was no thought process behind anything, no pause to think about the consequences of our actions. I was engulfed in it all, the passion, the intensity, her. It was like nothing I'd ever experienced and, before I knew it, the cubicle door was locked behind us, her body straddled over mine. My hands were lost in the curves of her body as I kissed her chest, her neck: Every inch of her was calling out to me; I couldn't get enough. She pushed back against me, her enthusiasm meeting mine. Our lips parted for a second, allowing me to look into her eyes for what felt like a lifetime before we retreated back to the ecstasy of our first kiss. I could taste her rawness; it was perfect as our tongues greeted one another, and my hands desperately pulled her closer.

There was a brief noise, we both went silent and the toilet door creaked as someone entered. She put her finger to my lips, forcing me to keep quiet as I tried to fight the urge to laugh. We'd found ourselves in an awkward situation; nobody wants to be the couple coming out of the toilet cubicle, looking sheepish.

We decided to keep quiet, wait it out. Once the bathroom stalls fell silent again, she reached for my face, pulling me in to resume the kiss. This time, it was more profound, with more meaning behind it. Imagine someone kissing you like they would never kiss you again - that's what it felt like; the desire was coursing through me.

After what must have been 20 minutes, Brooke elegantly stood from the straddling position she had found herself in, wiped the excess lipstick from around her mouth and placed her bag under her arm. I couldn't take my eyes off her.

"Do you think we are safe to leave?"

Neither of us had heard anything for a few minutes, so I nodded in agreement: The coast was clear.

As she went to open the cubicle, I pushed the door back into the frame and took her face between my hands one last time. She didn't resist. Instead, she welcomed the soft touch of my lips once again. It was like I had never kissed anyone before her as if my lips and my tongue had been made to meet hers. The rhythm in which they moved together was almost as if they'd been waiting for that moment, for her. She pushed me away with a playful gleam in her eyes, indicating that it was time to go.

"I think it's time we caught that train home, don't you?"

It was getting late, but I longed for the night to continue.

"I agree. After you."

I wondered if anyone would suspect our goings-on, given that I was undoubtedly a little more flustered than I had been prior to entering the bathroom.

We both stood, waiting for the train. Things started to get a little awkward the longer we waited, neither of us knowing how to address what had just transpired. It certainly took me by surprise, so I dread to think what Brooke was thinking. After all, to my knowledge, she had never kissed another woman before.

The train journey was a relatively quick one. Brooke got off a few stops before me. She caressed my hand before leaving, whispering, "I'll speak to you tomorrow."

That touch alone made me excited; her words left me hoping that she wouldn't regret anything that had happened. I put my earphones in and recalled the night's events over and over in my head. I couldn't shake the rush of excitement it gave me, my heart pounding the whole way to Soho. Poor Jake had been waiting longer than expected, so the drinks were most certainly on me.

It was 11 am before I woke from a night of much-needed sleep. I had collapsed into bed shortly after midnight; all I could think about was Brooke, which caused my mind to run away with itself. I hadn't fallen asleep until a few hours later. I was thankful I had the day off work.

I could tell that it was cold outside. The air was crisp and the heating wasn't on, which meant I wasn't getting out from under my duvet anytime soon. I had put my winter duvet on the weekend before, even treating myself to a new duvet cover and a few more pillows for the colder months. My bed needed to be comfortable and warm; I couldn't cope with being cold.

All I could think about was the night before, but I was disappointed to see no text from Brooke. I didn't know what to expect, but I was hoping she would let me know she didn't regret it or even better that she had enjoyed it. Anything that would make me feel like we hadn't just made a huge mistake.

I felt a buzz that morning, a feeling I hadn't experienced in years, the kind of euphoria that comes at the beginning of a relationship when you're getting to know each other, when everything is new and exciting.

The feeling was also a scary one because with it came the overwhelming fear of rejection, the fear of feelings not being mutual or that things might not pan out the way you thought they would.

I thought I would give it another hour before biting the bullet and texting her first. She could still be sleeping, or she could be thinking the same thing as me and not wanting to seem too keen.

Unfortunately, the world was one of heartbreak, so much so that it was hard for people to be vulnerable; nobody wants to seem like they are not in control. That's why so many relationships start the wrong way because the people involved are too scared to lose control.

I was thinking of a witty message that would be light-hearted enough but, as I was about to type, a message came through: She had made the first move.

Last night was amazing. I can't stop thinking about it, just so you know.

My heart started racing again; the grin that emerged from ear to ear was impossible to control. It was incredible how one text could make you feel a hundred different things. Because she had text first, I could now delve a little deeper, reassured by the fact that she made it clear she didn't regret it, making me happier than I had been in a very long time.

It was, wasn't it? What exactly can you not stop thinking about?

I couldn't help but be flirtatious. I wanted to know everything; what exactly had gone through her head, how she felt about me, about the kiss. I had to know.

You, your lips, your smell, your eyes, basically everything that involves you. How can one kiss make me feel this way? This morning, I feel like a silly schoolgirl that's never had a crush before.

She told me absolutely everything I had hoped she would.

I don't know, but I feel exactly the same way. It took me hours to get to sleep last night. All I could think about was kissing you again. Meet me today? Please?

I had to see her. Surely, if she felt the same way, she would want to see me too.

You certainly don't have to say please. There is no persuading needed here. Tell me when and where.

I couldn't reply quick enough.

Dinner at The White Horse near me? 2 pm this afternoon okay for you? They do an amazing carvery; you'll be impressed.

Her reply.

Sounds incredible, see you there.

I jumped out of bed, the cold suddenly not bothering me anymore, a spring in my step once again. I had a couple of hours to get ready, just enough time to shower and make sure I was looking my best but, most importantly, smelling my best. Her text referring to my smell meant that the gallons of perfume I sprayed every day of my life hadn't gone unnoticed. I had to smell good; it was one thing I made sure of.

The White Horse was the first pub that came to mind. It was close by, always busy and had never let me down in terms of the standard of food they served. They had nice, quiet booths that were sat away from the main bar area where the majority of people would congregate on a Sunday afternoon. It made things a little more intimate, which meant we could talk without prying ears or getting drowned out by the rowdy men watching the football.

I never did understand the hype when it came to football. My dad had tried to get me involved at a young age, but I had no interest whatsoever. There weren't many sports I enjoyed, Tennis and Formula One were about the only two, but everyone I knew seemed to think they were the most boring. Maybe I was just a boring person.

The clock was ticking. I knew it would only take me ten minutes to walk over to The White Horse, which gave me approximately 30 minutes to get ready. I was feeling rather posh in my outfit choice for the day. I put on my skinniest pair of black jeans, some black ankle boots, a white shirt and my grey, herringbone coat. A layering of accessories was a must considering it was almost freezing outside, so I added a black scarf and some gloves. I almost broke out the earmuffs but decided against it and wore my hair down so my ears would feel less like they were about to drop off.

There Brooke was, already waiting when I arrived, looking just as incredible as the night before. Her hair was still perfectly wavy, her make-up was more minimalistic, but that just made her even more beautiful. She had a similar outfit on; skinny black jeans, a beige turtleneck jumper and a long, black trench coat.

She smiled when she clocked me walking towards the table. I hadn't seen that smile before; it was different somehow, more genuine than it had been previously. She was shy; I could tell by the way she held herself, by the way she looked sheepishly away from me after I smiled back. She began to play with her hair, curling it around her finger.

There was already two drinks on the table as I got closer. One looked like a latte, perfect.

"I'm glad you're here; your drink's getting cold. I ordered you a latte. I see you have one almost every morning at work, so I figured it was the easiest option… Hello, by the way."

What was it about this girl? She made me so nervous. I didn't even know what to say.

"Hello again. Thank you for that; this will absolutely do the trick. It's freezing outside, isn't it? How long have you been sat here? I hope I didn't keep you waiting too long."

I knew I was on time. In fact, I was seven minutes early.

"I can't bring myself to take my coat off just yet; that's why I ordered us hot drinks. It's awful out there. Not too long, only five minutes or so, I always like to be early."

She put her perfectly pouted lips to her cup, touching the edge ever so slightly, taking a sip of what I assumed was hot chocolate. I couldn't help but laugh when she lowered her cup, and a tiny spot of whipped cream remained at the end of her nose. I reached for the napkin underneath my saucer to hand it over to her.

"You might want to get that unless you're saving it for later."

She leaned forward ever so slightly.

"You get it for me."

Brooke looked directly into my eyes. The way she spoke did something to me; it moved me in a way that my mind couldn't process. I didn't say a word. I just reached my hand over and carefully wiped the cream from her nose. The whole time, we didn't break eye contact. I wanted to kiss her again; the urge was uncontrollable. She leaned back in her seat and smiled; the conversation continued as normal.

We spoke for hours, long after the food had been and gone, three drinks later, and we were still chatting about anything and everything. I wasn't sure when was the right time to bring the date to a close; I hadn't even called it a date. I wasn't really sure what it was. All I knew was I wanted to be around her for as long as possible, and the thought of her going home saddened me.

"I better go home soon, Holly. My dad will be wondering where I am."

My heart sank. I was hoping it didn't have to come to an end so soon.

"That's fine, I understand. I have kept you talking long enough."

She smiled and touched my hand from across the table.

"I have enjoyed every second of being here with you, as sad as that may sound. I wish I could stay longer, but I have to be in by 7 pm on a Sunday, family tradition."

I felt warm inside; her words had made me happy. I was unsure why she had to be in by 7 pm, I thought it was a bit strange and it wasn't something she had mentioned before, but

I was positive she was too old to be having a curfew. I didn't want to pry, but equally, I wanted to know.

"I'm glad because I have enjoyed it too. I'm sad you have to go. I feel like there's so much more we could talk about. Do you have a curfew or something? Don't tell me you have a criminal conviction. I didn't expect that of you, Brooke."

I winked as I said the last bit, making it clear that I was joking, trying to be light-hearted about the situation whilst getting her to open up slightly and reveal the reason at the same time.

"I don't, cheeky! It may sound weird, it's not usually something I speak about, but you know my mum passed away four years ago. I told you that, didn't I?"

She had never mentioned that, which took me by surprise. I could have sworn she mentioned her mum once and it wasn't in the past tense, but I was obviously wrong. I was shocked because we had spoken so much lately and it was never something that fell into conversation, although it wouldn't be the first thing I opted to talk about either.

"No, I don't think you did. I'm sorry, that's awful, Brooke. I'm surprised you never told me."

I didn't want her to feel like she had to tell me, but at the same time, I didn't want her to feel like she couldn't.

"I think I've told you more about myself than I have anyone over these past few weeks, so I'm surprised I didn't. It's a difficult subject for me but, basically, every Sunday we used to sit around the table as a family and have our usual roast dinner. We would talk about our weekend, what we were looking forward to in the week at school or work.

We had a routine, as we had done since I was born. We would have dinner around 7; then dessert would always be around 8. I would beg for cheesecake or strawberry trifle every week, but everyone else usually wanted the same old chocolate cake. I was outnumbered on most occasions, but I grew to love it.

Anyway, after dessert, we would spend an hour playing chess. We had two boards, so my brother would play my dad, and I would play my mum, and then we would swap. It's kind of silly, but we enjoyed it; we even had a scoreboard up in the dining room. This scoreboard would go on for an entire year and then whoever won would get a special treat on New Year's Day. Some years, the treat was amazing. I won three years in a row once and, each time, I asked for a trip to Disneyland Paris. I was only like 12 years old, so as you can imagine, that was all I wanted to do at the time."

Brooke raised her cup to her lips to drink the remnants of her hot chocolate, smiling sweetly at the memories of her childhood.

"On the second year, my mum said how sorry she was, but they couldn't afford for us to go. I understood because I think I was at the age were money started to mean something. I had realised it didn't grow on trees and I couldn't have absolutely everything I wanted.

By the third year, I didn't ask again and, instead, I asked if I could just have a new pair of trainers I wanted because all my friends had them. The next day, my mum came home with the trainers and a brochure for Disneyland Paris. I started crying when she told me we could go in April that year, and I couldn't contain my excitement. I told anyone and everyone that would listen. After my mum passed, I later found out that she and my dad had rigged the scores that year so that I would win again and they could surprise me with the trip. She had saved up for a full two years to be able to take us all there. I loved her so much for that."

She was absently tugging the strands of her hair that fell

across her chest, almost losing her train of thought before she snapped back to reality.

"I know I'm babbling on now, so I will get to the point. I guess I have never had the heart to tell my dad that I couldn't make it to Sunday evenings anymore. I almost feel like we're keeping my mum's memory alive. She always made sure we were a close-knit family. Even through the years when my dad was working away in the Army, she would tell him he had to call on a Sunday night at nine, so we could tell him who had won. I know it's probably not something I can keep up forever, but me and my brother both try our best, just for my dad's sake, more than anything. He still really struggles with the loss of her. I still hear him crying every now and again; it's heart-breaking."

I could see a tear forming in the corner of her eye and I felt her pain. It was awful, losing a loved one. I didn't want her to feel uncomfortable about telling me.

I thought it was honourable, the way she loved her father, the way she wanted to help her mother's memory live on.

"Don't ever say that it's silly, Brooke. What you've just told me was beautiful and honourable and I would do exactly the same thing if I were in your shoes. It's nice to have a family that's so close. You need that support around you, especially in the hardest times. I want you to know that I'm deeply sorry that you had to go through that. Can I ask how she passed away?"

She wiped the corner of her eye, and I reached for her hand to give it a small, compassionate squeeze, letting her know it was okay to be emotional; we are only human.

"She passed away suddenly; it was a shock to us all. I think that's what made it even harder, having no time to say goodbye or to do the things that she'd always wanted to do. She was only 45. It was a brain aneurysm, a severe one. Apparently, they can go undetected for a long time so we were completely unaware there was anything wrong. It was a rare case and there was absolutely nothing that could've been done. I try and reassure myself that she didn't suffer; she passed away in her sleep. It would've been selfish of me to wish something else upon her so that I could've had longer with her. It was the hardest day of my life; it's still unbearably hard."

I could see the pain etched across her face, but there were no words I could say that would bring her mother back, no words that would even ease the hurt. Grief is, and always will be, a horrible feeling; it destroys the very best of us.

"I can only imagine how hard it must've been for you, how hard it still is. All we hope for when we lose a loved one is that they go peacefully. Nobody wants to see the one they love suffer and, although she was taken incredibly young, you must take some peace from that, as hard as it may be."

She nodded in silent agreement.

"Thank you. You're so easy to talk to; that's one of the things I like about you."

She looked down at her watch; it was time for her to leave.

"Do you want me to walk you to the station?"

I was trying to prolong the time spent with her for as long as I possibly could.

"I would really like that, yes. Isn't it in the opposite direction to where you live, though? I don't want you going out of your way."

It was roughly five minutes in the opposite direction from my house but I didn't care. The extra few minutes with her was worth the longer walk home, even in the freezing cold.

"It's no trouble at all. Would it be uncool if I said I am just happy to talk with you a little longer?"

There was that smile again.

"Totally uncool, but I'll let you off."

She was incredibly witty and I adored that.

Brooke gathered her belongings, retrieved a bobble hat from her bag and very delicately pulled it over her head.

The walk to the station was over quickly. The cold had made the walk less of a pleasant stroll and more of a speed walk. Before I knew it, it was time to say goodbye.

"When will I see you again? Shall we do something maybe Wednesday?"

Brooke looked deep in thought for a second before responding.

"I'd like that. Shall I choose the place this time?"

My inner self was secretly doing backflips at the prospect of seeing her again, even if I had to wait nearly three full days.

"Of course, that sounds perfect. Let me know a place and a time, and I will see you there. You better go; you'll miss the train."

I wasn't sure what was an appropriate goodbye gesture. I extended my arms out for a hug and she embraced me straight away with no hesitation, her head fitting perfectly just below my chin as she cuddled into my neck. I was above average height, which had its advantages.

Neither one of us wanted to let go and, just when I thought the time was right, she held on just a little while longer. She lifted her head and kissed me softly on my cheek as she pulled away, the feeling lingering for several minutes after her lips left. Brooke smiled that beautiful smile and walked away, looking back every few steps just to check I was still watching. She left me wanting more every single time I came into contact with her.

I was captivated.

CHAPTER TWELVE

It was Wednesday 19th December and the smile on my face was just as big as it had been all week. My work colleagues and friends had started to notice the change in my behaviour; *'You seem happy again'*, they would say or *'who's put that smile on your face'*. I kept quiet about the whole situation, of course, as I knew Brooke wasn't ready to talk about what was going on to anyone other than me. It was hard to hide my obvious excitement every time I saw her face, but I tried to keep my feelings under wraps. Every night that we stayed up talking that little bit longer, every time she divulged new information about her life or her hobbies or her family, I liked her that little bit more.

The night before, we spoke about Christmas, how much we loved the winter season because it brought so much fun with Halloween, Bonfire night, Christmas and New year. It was a season that took a severe toll on my bank balance but still one that I enjoyed nevertheless. The big day was a mere six days away. I thought about getting Brooke a present, unsure if that would put too much pressure on the situation or make her feel she had to get me one. I didn't want that; I wasn't the type to buy people presents so that I would receive them in return. I was a nightmare for buying everything I wanted when I wanted it so, when it came to Christmas, people would always struggle with what to get me. It's the thought that counts, and I truly believed that.

The funny thing was, I already knew what I would get her. She was a massive fan of Disney/Pixar movies, I don't think there was one she hadn't watched. I knew this because she spoke about them constantly, and the majority of the time, when I asked her what she was doing, it was usually watching a Disney film. I had seen a Lion King cup and a Disney notebook with all the movies on the cover, which I thought she would love.

There hadn't been a minute since we kissed that we hadn't been in contact. I remember, some days, practically falling asleep at work because we'd stayed up until the early hours of the morning, talking about everything and nothing at all. Every morning, the first name that appeared on my phone was Brooke; just her simple *'Good Morning'* was all it took to start my day off perfectly.

The phone rang as I sat eating my breakfast. I was surprised at the name that appeared on the screen, so I answered hesitantly.

"Hi, Lucy, this is a surprise."

Lucy was an old friend. I had known her for a very long time, but we often drifted apart and then back together again. I had always known Lucy liked me, but the feeling had never been mutual: She was high maintenance, extremely hard work and thought the whole world revolved around her. Despite all that, we had always been friends because she was different with me; she cared for my happiness and kept her own feelings bottled up.

Lucy often got drunk and told me exactly how she felt, which made things somewhat awkward when I was with Danielle because she also knew about Lucy's feelings. I didn't see the problem because I didn't reciprocate the feelings; therefore, everything was utterly platonic and friendly from my point of view. I understood that was not the case for Danielle.

It had been at least nine months since we last spoke, and to be honest, I was expecting a phone call or a text message from her after my split from Danielle, especially now that it was common knowledge. It had been challenging to remain friends with her whilst I was with Danielle. It was difficult for her too because she felt the uneasiness every time we were all in the same room and, if there was one thing I hated, it was awkwardness.

Her voice was as chirpy as ever when she replied.

"Hi, Holly! How are you? I know this is completely random, but I was just sat at home and I saw your name on my Facebook newsfeed and I just thought I'd give you a call. I know it's been a while."

If she was anything, it was random.

"I'm really good, thank you, are you? I was surprised to see your name pop up. It has been about a year, hasn't it?"

"More like nine months, but who's counting. I'm glad to hear it. I heard about your recent break-up. I'm sorry to hear that, but I can't say I am surprised. I never really did see eye-to-eye with Danielle, I always thought you could do a lot better, but we won't get into that. I have some news, anyway."

She was certainly counting by the sounds of things. I knew she would get a sly dig in there about Danielle if she could. I was shocked that I hadn't heard at all from Lucy in the immediate weeks after the break-up.

"Oh, really, what's the news? Please, tell me you've won the lottery and you're calling to share the winnings."

She laughed, briefly paused and then continued.

"No, it's even better than that. I'll give you one more guess."

I had no idea what it could be, but I took a wild stab in the dark.

"I don't know, you've got a new job? You're moving away? You got a puppy?"

I was all out of guesses, and quite frankly, I wasn't really that interested.

"Okay, that was terrible, Holly. First of all, none of those things are better than winning the lottery – well, maybe the puppy, but I already have 2 of those, so no need for a third…I have a girlfriend!!!"

Lucy bellowed the last bit down the phone as if it was earth-shattering news. I knew she had been in relationships before, so it wasn't as though she had been single for a long time and this was a miracle.

"Wow, that's great. How long have you been together?"

I wasn't really sure what else to say.

"We have been official for about five months now. She's great; I'm really happy."

That would explain why she was, all of a sudden, off the radar. I hadn't seen much of her out and about or on Facebook for the few months prior. I'm glad she was happy; she deserved that. She was a good girl, underneath the loud persona she carried.

"That's amazing, Lucy. I'm really happy for you. Do I know her?"

There was a brief pause that kept me in suspense.

"You may have seen her out and about. I don't think you know her, though. Her name is Chloe Aria."

The name didn't ring a bell.

"I don't know, possibly. How did you meet?"

"We met on a night out. I'd spoken to her a few times before, but we were always seeing other people, so nothing ever happened. What about you? No new love interests?"

I wasn't about to divulge all the details of whatever it was Brooke and me were doing.

"No, nothing going on with me. I'm quite happy to be single for a while."

It was true. I didn't want to rush into anything with Brooke; I didn't want to get ahead of myself.

"That's probably the right thing to do. Take your time and find the right person. What are you up to today?"

"Not a lot, just seeing a friend this afternoon. You?"

I didn't have anything else to do other than see Brooke.

"I'm over your way seeing my sister this afternoon, so I was just wondering if you wanted to catch up but, if you've already got plans, maybe another time?"

"That's a shame. We could do it another day. It might have to be after Christmas, though. I'm going to be so busy at work until the holiday break."

That wasn't a lie by any stretch of the imagination. I was about to get swept up in the Christmas rush over the next week, so my social life was about to become non-existent.

"Okay, well, how about I text you in the New Year? Maybe we could meet up then? I'd really like you to meet Chloe; I think you'd get along really well."

"That sounds great; I'm sure we can arrange something. If I don't speak to you before, have a great Christmas."

"Thank you, you too. Take care. Bye."

"Bye, Lucy."

The phone went silent. That was a very random conversation – my initial thought. It was nice of her to check in, but I was still expecting her to want something or have some ulterior motive.

My phone had been busier than usual that morning. I came off the phone to Lucy to find three unread text messages.

The only one that interested me was Brooke's. There was another from my parents asking what time I would be over on Christmas day and a message from Danielle. I hadn't heard from her in a while, so it was a shock to the system to see the name pop up on my screen.

The message read:

Hi, Holly, I just wanted to say that I hope you have a fantastic Christmas. I'm going to see my Uncle in Spain this year. It will be hard for me not to do our usual routine, so I think it's best to get away and clear my head. I just want you to know I'll be thinking about you and I still wish things could've been different. I love you. I always will. Take care.

There was an awful pain in my chest every time I read a message like that. I knew how much she would be hurting, and I knew she would probably be crying whilst she wrote the message, thinking about all the Christmases we had spent together. I wanted to let her know I still cared, but it was difficult; I didn't want to make things even harder for her or give her any false hope.

Hi, Danielle, thank you. I really appreciate that. I hope you have a lovely Christmas. I think that will be good for you, a change of scenery is always good. For what it's worth, I wish things could've been different too. I'll never forget our time together and please don't ever think I don't care. Take care of yourself. I'm here if you need me.

I wasn't sure what else to say. I couldn't bring myself to tell her I loved her because, the truth was, I didn't. I had fallen out of love with Danielle a long time ago. All that remained now was an obligation to care for her, which I always would.

Finally, I clicked on Brooke's message. The first word I saw was 'sorry' and my heart sank. I instantly thought she had cancelled our plans that afternoon until I read a little further on.

Sorry, but there has been a change of plans. I want us to go for a nice walk instead, so make sure you wrap up. It's not quite as cold as it has been, but it's cold enough. The sun is out though, and this place is beautiful. I'll pick you up in my dad's car around 3, be ready.

A change of plans was better than a cancelling of plans. I didn't even know what the change of plans had been, it was all a surprise and that excited me. I quickly replied before throwing on some clothes so I could head to the shops.

I didn't have long left to get the last of my Christmas presents. Every year, all of a sudden, it seemed like we hit September and the rest was a blur. That year was no different. I knew exactly what I needed, so it should've made for a relatively quick and easy trip. However, it was a week before Christmas so why I thought the underground would be quiet and the high street stores would have everything I needed was beyond me. I had approximately two hours before I needed to head home to give myself enough time to get changed and freshen up for my afternoon with Brooke.

The shops were not about to hold me prisoner. I knew exactly what I wanted, so I was in and out with no hesitation; the only thing I didn't manage to purchase was a dressing gown for my grandma. She had to have a particular one and she wasn't the type to hold her tongue if she ended up with the wrong one.

I arrived home shortly before 2 pm, entered my apartment and headed straight for the spare room. There, I dumped the six bags of presents amongst those already wrapped and the mountains of gifts with still no definite recipient.

I had a problem when it came to buying gifts. I would purchase the odd thing here or there, simply because I thought it would be a nice gift for someone, then decide on Christmas Eve who the presents would go to. On the odd occasion, some of them would stay with me.

The weather outside was a perfect mix of winter and summer. The sky was blue, and the sun was shining but the cold, winter air made for cold hands and cold ears. I was unsure what to wear, but I figured I needed to wrap up, as instructed.

My phone vibrated on my dressing table just as I was finishing up spraying my last bit of perfume and checking my hair was poker straight (the bits you could see poking out from underneath my hat anyway). I had opted for a black hat, scarf and glove set I'd purchased the year before and still hadn't worn.

"Here" was all the text read, followed by kisses. I re-adjusted my hat one last time and grabbed my bag on the way out.

There she was, waiting patiently, looking up and waving as I approached. Her dad's car was nice, a black Audi Q7. I knew that her dad had a decent job, but I had never pried too much into what he did or ask about his wage. I just know that he had nice cars, and they lived in a large, contemporary home so I assumed it was a hefty sum.

"Hey, you could've given me a 5-minute warning."

"What do you need that for? You got down here pretty fast; I assumed you'd only be looking at yourself in the mirror." She laughed.

"Very funny. This car is really nice. How did you convince your dad to let you drive this?"

I knew my parents and I knew they would not let me drive their pride and joy for fear I would break it. You would think that, at the age of 28, they would've started to have a little faith in me not ruining things.

"I'm his only daughter. Without sounding spoilt, I get pretty much whatever I want. Besides, he has three cars, and he can't use them all at the same time. He insured me on all three because he trusts me, unlike my brother. Six months after he passed his test, my dad trusted him with his brand new BMW. He only went and smashed it straight into the gate, didn't even get off the street."

I couldn't help but laugh. So, it seemed she was a daddy's girl. She didn't come across like that when I spoke to her but it was apparent that she had his heart.

"Well, you're lucky. Why do I feel like you live in a huge, gated mansion and your father is the King of a faraway land? What does he do, anyway, for work?" There was a slight hesitation, almost like she didn't want to tell me.

"We don't live in a gated mansion as such; we do have a gate though. It's only a five-bedroom house and it's lovely, don't get me wrong, but I don't get attached to houses anymore. I moved that much as a child. In answer to your question, he is a Management Consultant for a big firm, overseas. I don't pry too much into his work life because he's stressed a lot. The benefits and the wage may be good, but I'm not sure it's worth all the hassle."

I remember instantly feeling like her father would be the type of man you wouldn't want to get on the wrong side of and I didn't even know him.

"Only five bedrooms? Wow, you're hard done to, princess."

She hit me playfully as we continued a drive to a destination that was still unknown to me.

"Why did you move so much? Is that because of your dad's job?"

I couldn't help but wonder how people got into those types of jobs, the ones with the big salaries and the company benefits. I'm guessing he must've been clever or a bit dodgy. I was hoping for the former.

"Yes. Basically, he goes where his firm wants him to go. They're expanding every year, they get new business somewhere and they always want him to go. They offer him more money and a nice house abroad, all the benefits you could imagine. Who wouldn't take it? My mum loved seeing different countries, learning about different cultures and it was fascinating until me and my brother started to get a little older. We wanted to stay in the same place because we'd made friends and it was always hard, uprooting your life all over again. I think the longest I stayed in one place was five years, and I've been back in England for six years now, but I'm still scared to get the phone call off my dad saying it's time to go."

She'd previously told me that her life had been hectic as a kid, that she'd been moved from pillar to post, but I was never under the impression that she would move again.

"Wow, I bet it was amazing, though, as a child, to experience that. Do you think you'd go with him then if they told him he had to move again?"

She paused. It was clearly something she'd thought about.

"I would have to. He needs us around him and I genuinely believe he would drive himself insane if he didn't have my brother and me. I spoke to him about it earlier this year, but he wasn't sure whether he would take another opportunity to move away again. He doesn't have to do it, they won't fire him if he said no, but he always feels obliged to take every opportunity. I guess I'm similar, in that sense, I'm terrible at saying 'no'."

It was admirable the way she loved her father. She was willing to be there for him no matter what, even if it meant putting her own life on hold.

"Being terrible at saying 'no' isn't always a bad thing. At least you experience the most out of life. So, if you don't mind me asking, why on earth do you work at West & Hayes? I can't imagine they pay you well as an intern. It seems like you don't need to work, and surely your dad could get you a well-paid job. You're clever enough; that's clear to see."

She exhaled, and her expression said a thousand words.

"I want my own independence. My dad has money, but he's not a millionaire. I won't inherit a billion-dollar company that will let me lead a lavish lifestyle, much to my dismay. My dad has tried to get me into his business. I witnessed so many business meetings when I was younger, and I always thought I wanted to be like 'Daddy'. Then I saw the toll it took on his life and his relationships with friends and family. It's hard, always having to put your career first, and I don't want that. No amount of money is worth that, but my dad loves it; it's the only thing that keeps him from tipping over the edge. He has a career that takes up the majority of his time and, when it doesn't, his children do, and that's how he lives his life."

She spoke about her father with such passion. It was clear to see how much she respected him and loved him for the life he had given her, her brother, and of course, her mother before her passing. It made me wonder how long she would feel as though she was indebted to him.

"He sounds like an honourable man."

The car fell silent for several seconds and then the subject was swiftly changed.

"So, you've not even asked where we are going? Are you not a little intrigued? I could be kidnapping you."

"The thought had crossed my mind, but you don't seem like the kidnapping type, so I'm not worried just yet. Where are we going?"

"We are going for a walk through Cliveden's Country Estate. It's a beautiful place to walk, have you ever been?"

The name stood out, but I couldn't be sure if I'd ever been or not. I wasn't one for walking; it was a rarity that I would go for a leisurely walk simply because I wanted to. I chose not to tell Brooke that. I didn't want her to think I would dislike the idea.

"I don't think so. What's it like?"

"It's just beautiful. The trees, the flowers, the gardens, they are so immaculately kept, even in the winter. About half-way around, there's a wonderful view over the River Thames, and if we're lucky, we might even see some deer. I used to walk there all the time when I was a child, but it's been such a long time since I last went."

"It sounds great. How far away is it?"

We had already been driving for about 15 minutes.

"It's about 40 minutes. It's difficult to find beautiful places to walk so close to London. If you haven't noticed, there is no such thing as the countryside where we live."

She gave me a look; I knew that look.

"You love giving me that look, don't you? You're so sarcastic sometimes. I'm not going to lie though; I quite like it."

We both laughed.

"I can't control my facial reactions; you know that."

There was something about her confidence that sucked me in. I was ultimately out of control in her presence, but it didn't scare me. If anything, it spurred me on, made me want to see how far we could go.

We finally arrived, precisely 47 minutes later. I could see a barn and trees that ran for miles. I noticed a narrow pathway through an archway of green bushes, and I assumed that was where we would begin our walk.

"It's through here. I know it doesn't look like much right now, but it comes to life as you walk around."

We took in the scenery as we walked. We didn't need to talk constantly; sometimes, it was nice to hear nothing but the birdsong. She had been right, though, not that I doubted her for a minute. The place was beautiful.

"What do you think, Holly?"

Her ears were waiting for approval.

"I think it's something special. Thank you for bringing me here."

"You are welcome. I mean, it's kind of a cheap date, isn't it? I just had to drive 40 minutes."

Did she just refer to our trip out as a date? It took a second to register.

"Did you just call this a date? I'm sure I heard the word 'date'."

"Shut up, you idiot. You know what I mean."

She playfully pushed me away. I'd clearly embarrassed her.

"I'm joking. I know what you mean. Is that what you think we're doing now? Dating?"

She looked around, biding time until she found the right words.

"Well, I don't know, are we not? I mean, I would say so."

I don't think I'd ever seen her so nervous.

"I'd like to think so. Without putting too much pressure on the situation, I'm certainly not talking to anyone else if that means anything to you."

She was surprised.

"Why do I not believe you? I mean, look at you. I see how much attention you get."

I was flattered and wanted to smile, but I tried to remain serious. I wanted her to know I wasn't like that.

"Just because I get attention, that doesn't mean anything. I've seen the attention you get from men on a night out. Does that mean you're entertaining it? No."

"Fair point, I just can't explain it. We have kissed once, and yes, it was amazing, but does that warrant you not talking to other people? I don't know. I guess I wouldn't blame you if you were."

All I focused on was the word 'amazing'.

"Can I kiss you again? I know it's a little off subject, but I just really want to kiss you again."

I was done fighting the urge. I didn't care where we were at that moment. I just wanted to relive the night in the underground, just for a second. We both stopped and she looked up into my eyes, nodding slowly.

"I'd love that."

The world around us suddenly fell away. The walk wasn't busy on a Wednesday afternoon, but I didn't stop to take a look at who was around or if they may have found it inappropriate. I didn't care.

I moved in closer and placed my hands on either side of her face; she then placed her hands around my waist. I could tell she felt self-conscious when I looked into her eyes, but we were both unable to look away. Her flawless skin and clear, brown eyes were perfect; the sprinkle of freckles across her nose and her gorgeous, blonde hair glistened in the winter sun. I couldn't help but wonder if Brooke's heart was beating as fast as mine and if she felt anything close to the desire burning in my stomach.

I gently placed my lips on hers, instantly hungry for more. Her hands tightened around my waist as she pulled herself in closer. The tip of her tongue brushed my lips so softly, her mouth insistent. I embraced every second of her touch. Everything around us fell oddly silent, like there was nobody else in the vicinity, only Brooke and me. I felt like every other kiss I had been a part of had been wrong, incomparable to the way I felt at that moment.

Her fingers slipped up to the back of my neck and then into the hair underneath my hat; she gripped my hair fiercely and pulled my lips harder onto her own. I was breathless, swept up in the moment and I loved it.

She pulled away just before the exchange got a little too heated. We had to come back to reality and remember exactly where we were. We both looked around us, checking that we hadn't just been partaking in a heavily-watched public display of affection. Luckily, there was only one man close by, and he didn't seem to bat an eyelid as he walked on with his Yorkshire Terrier in tow. Neither of us spoke, but the looks on our faces said a thousand words.

Brooke reached for my hand as we continued down the long and windy path ahead. Her hand fit perfectly in mine as if it had been made just for me.

Although the sun was still shining, the weather had dropped off; it was only 4 degrees outside. Thankfully, it was the inside of Brooke's dad's car that was telling me the temperature. The walk had lasted around two hours. It was peaceful, all in all, an excellent way to spend the afternoon.

The heating was on full power as we continued the drive back. The conversation was flowing - as it always was - there was such ease when I spoke to Brooke. I never had to think about what to say next; things just came to me so naturally. I was toying with the idea of asking her upstairs to my apartment because I didn't want the day to end but, before I had the chance to ask, she had a phone call from her dad. It came through the hands-free system in the car.

"Hi, sweetheart, when are you going to be home?"

Brooke hesitated before she answered.

"Shouldn't be too much longer, Dad. I'm just driving back from Cliveden's. Why is everything alright?"

"It's fine. I could just do with the car this evening. I'm taking the fellas to the game. You know I can't squeeze them into the Jag."

"Okay, dad, that's okay. I'll be back in the next 40 minutes or so."

There was a pause on the line before he continued.

"Cliveden's as in where we used to walk with your mum when you were younger? Who've you gone there with?"

His voice was chirpy, but you could hear the uncertain curiosity.

"Yes, Dad, that's the one. Just with my friend Holly, from work."

She kept it short and sweet.

"Okay, well, I hope you had a nice afternoon. Say 'hello' to Holly for me, and I will see you when you get home."

"Will do. See you later, Dad."

The phone line went dead, and there was an uneasiness in the air. She looked slightly panicked and I wasn't sure why.

"Are you okay? Does your father not like it when you don't tell him where you're going?"

That's certainly the impression I was getting.

"Of course, I'm fine. I don't tell him everything. He can just be hard work sometimes, that's all. I'm an adult; I shouldn't have to check in with my dad all the time. Unfortunately, he tightened the reigns a hell of a lot after my mum died."

"Surely, he must understand you have your own life? Don't take this the wrong way, but it seems to me like you spend the majority of your time keeping your dad happy. Are you ever going to start living for you?"

It was probably unfair of me to say that last part. I understood, from what she'd told me, that her dad needed her, but at the same time, he should be letting his daughter live her own life.

"I do live for me, Holly. You've known me for a few months, and that's a snapshot of my life. Don't judge something you don't know an awful lot about."

I was shocked by her abruptness and she could sense that.

"I'm sorry, I didn't mean to sound rude."

"I'm sorry too. I just don't want you to judge him; he's been through a lot."

Her love for her dad was as apparent as ever.

"I guess I'm just sorry you have to go home. I was hoping you could have spent the evening with me."

Brooke pulled the car onto my street. I was sad because my time with her always ended too quickly.

"Maybe another time? I'm afraid after that kiss, I might not have been able to control myself and I am a lady, you know."

The thought of her not being able to control herself sent shivers down my spine. I wanted her so badly, but I knew I'd have to wait.

"I'll hold you to that. Have a safe drive home. Text me later, yeah?"

There was no doubt in my mind that she would, and I would wait in anticipation, as I had done every day prior.

"I will, come here."

I leaned over and felt her lips on mine once again. I needed her lips like a vampire required blood. I climbed out of the car and waved her goodbye from the pavement.

My bed awaited for me to retire for the evening. I planned to eat unhealthy food, watch terribly made romantic comedies and talk to Brooke for the whole evening. My life had become a simple one, but I would quickly learn that nothing ever stayed simple for very long.

CHAPTER THIRTEEN

"How do you feel about meeting my dad?"

The question took me by surprise. It was Christmas Eve and I was walking down Oxford Street with the phone to my ear. The snow was falling and I could hear Christmas music playing.

"Really? I mean, are you sure? When?"

I was baffled, to say the least. I think the surprise in my voice was more obvious than I meant it to be.

"Calm down. I'm not about to throw you in at the deep end; even I'm not ready for whatever that would bring. I mentioned that I was seeing you Boxing Day night, and he was just curious as to who you are, considering I am spending a significant amount of time with you lately."

That made sense; the panic eased.

"Okay, that's fair enough. Won't that be awkward? I mean, I feel like that would be awkward, wouldn't it?"

"Holly, you're my friend. My dad has met all my friends. It will literally be a five-minute introduction before we head out, that's all."

She was extremely calm and collected about the whole thing. Maybe I was reading too much into it.

"So, I'm just your friend? Well, if that's the case then I guess I have nothing to worry about, do I?"

Winding Brooke up had become such a natural part of my day, bringing me great pleasure.

"You know what I mean! What else can I call you? If it makes you feel any better, I certainly have never felt this way about a friend."

There was that stomach flutter again.

"I know; I just like to tease you. Well, I agree with the above statement, just so you know."

She fell silent on the other end of the line.

"You're killing me here, speaking all these sweet nothings. How am I supposed to concentrate on wrapping all these presents?"

We both laughed. The conversation was always so light-hearted and innocent between us.

"I will leave you to your wrapping. I need to head back into the office. I have a busy few hours ahead before I can finally start to enjoy Christmas."

"I hope it goes quick. Text me later."

"Thanks, Brooke, I will."

I was just ready to hang up when she added.

"I bought a little something today for Boxing Day. Picture black, lace underwear with very little left for the imagination; maybe that will help you through the rest of the day. Bye, Holly."

Just like that, she was gone and I was left with excitement like no other. I didn't know what to expect when meeting her dad. He seemed like the type of man that controlled her life, but at the same time, he obviously loved his daughter unconditionally. I could only form an opinion from what I had seen and heard in the brief time I had been getting to know

Brooke. I would soon have a very clear first impression of my own.

The rest of the day flew by. You could tell that everyone was feeling festive, almost every single person wore a Christmas jumper and nearly every post on social media involved a Santa emoji. I was pre-occupied with thoughts of Christmas dinner, gin and Brooke's underwear. A strange combination but it kept me going, all the same.

The Christmas period had been a rather pleasant one. I was coming to the end of my 6th year working at the law firm, and it had become my way of living. I thrived off the high-paced environment.

Before I knew it, it was 4 pm and my day was done. I made a point of saying 'Merry Christmas' to all my colleagues before I left, giving each a bottle of bubbly. Although it wasn't much, it was a gesture I felt would be greatly appreciated after another year packed with long hours and sleepless nights. They never expected anything, just as I didn't, and I could see the appreciation on their faces. That, alone, made my Christmas.

I also didn't leave empty-handed. I must have done something right that year because I got a few generous gifts. Amongst the usual chocolates and alcohol, I also got a new leather satchel for work with a matching phone case in a gorgeous, tan colour. I remember raving to one person in particular about how much I loved the bag, so I knew exactly who would've been behind the gift. I was extremely grateful and hugely taken aback by the gesture. It makes all the hours and the effort put in worthwhile knowing that people appreciate all you do.

I left work and walked briskly towards the underground with my old bag on my back and my new bag in hand. I quickly pulled my phone out to send a quick text to Brooke before placing my hands rapidly back in my coat pocket. It was a cold afternoon.

Once I arrived home, I hurled my belongings onto the bed and headed straight for the comfort of a warm bath. I had already gathered all my clothes and gifts together, so I was on the road within an hour. A four-hour road trip back home was never a quick one, but it was always an exciting drive, knowing I was going back to the place I came from. More importantly, I was excited to be back with my family, who would all be waiting eagerly for my arrival.

Christmas was always short and sweet as most of my family had jobs that required them to work over Christmas, meaning that the festivities never lasted longer than a day or two. Even so, I couldn't imagine spending it any other way.

I passed the time by calling a few of my friends, wishing them a 'Happy Christmas' and the rest of the trip was filled with my music playlists because there was absolutely no way that I was spending hours listening to Mariah Carey or The Pogues. By that point, I had heard quite enough of them.

Christmas didn't disappoint. I was spoilt rotten, as always, and the look on my mum's face when she opened her new YSL handbag was a picture I will never forget. She had always wanted a designer handbag but always opted for the cheap, high street option so she could spend more money on everyone else. I thought it was time to treat her to something she certainly deserved.

I received a very nice watch (which I loved), some pyjamas, perfume, chocolates, the usual bits, but none of that mattered. I was very much like my mum; I loved to give gifts rather than receive them. It was a much greater feeling, seeing someone else's happiness.

The day was over as quickly as it had begun. After all of that build-up - 364 days for just one day - it seemed a lot, but it was still something I would always look forward to. I hoped to pass the same excitement on to my own children someday.

Precisely 24 hours later and I was on the long drive back to London with one thing on my mind: Seeing Brooke. I hadn't spoken to her very much as she also had a busy schedule with her family, lots of people to see and not enough time. We had wished each other a 'Merry Christmas', given each other a brief overview of the day and what 'Santa' had brought for us, but that was the extent of it.

In the back of my mind, I had been watching the imaginary clock tick away, the hands growing closer and closer to when I would see her again. But it wouldn't just be Brooke this time; I would be meeting her dad as well. The thought of meeting her dad made me incredibly nervous, but I tried not to overthink the situation, telling myself that he would be lovely or, at least, I hoped.

The drive home was happily taken up by an hour-long conversation with Brooke.

"I'm looking forward to seeing you later, although I do have a bit of bad news."

My heart sank. I didn't like bad news when it came to Brooke.

"Oh, really, what's up?"

"I won't be able to stay over. I thought I might be able to swing it, but my dad's got all the family around, and he'd like me to at least show my face towards the end of the evening. I'm sorry, believe me, I'd much rather be spending the night with you."

I couldn't help but feel disappointed, given that I had a whole night planned.

"That's a shame. I was really looking forward to it. So, how long do I get the pleasure of your company then?"

She could probably hear the disappointment in my voice but I knew that seeing her, even if only for a few hours, was better than not at all.

"Me too, believe me, pick me up around 6? I'll need to be back for about 9, but it gives us time to catch up. I can think of a lot of things that can be achieved in 3 hours…"

There was a small pause on the line and, just like that, I was excited again.

"Oh, really? I was going to cook a nice tea, but maybe we should just grab food out if we don't have a lot of time? I'm easy, to be honest."

I enjoyed cooking and I was ready to show off my skills; it wasn't meant to be.

"Tea out sounds good to me. There's a nice pub near me we could try? It's fairly new but I've heard good things."

"Perfect, I'll see you at 6!"

I had 2 hours before I was due to see Brooke and briefly meet her father. That was the scary part. The more I got to know Brooke, the more I saw his influence over her and her willingness to keep him happy. All of which, potentially, would not go in my favour.

My eagerness meant I was ready a little too early, which was bad. It meant I had time to overthink things and get myself worked up, which was certainly not helping the situation. I played around with my hair some more, sprayed more perfume, ironed my t-shirt again – I had creased it by sitting down - I hated it when that happened.

After a good 30 minutes of biding my time, I climbed into my car and headed for Brooke's. I pulled up at precisely 6 pm, the gate was already open upon my arrival and there was no shortage of places to park. Even with three cars, the driveway had a great deal of space. I could see Brooke waving me in from the porch and, as I got closer, I couldn't help but grin from ear to ear. She looked incredible. She didn't even look like she'd tried to dress up, her make-up (as always) was understated and her hair was wavy and fell perfectly down the front of her body. I imagined her to be the type of girl that other girls envied, not because of what she wore or her facial features, simply because she didn't have to try and she could still turn heads.

We gave each other a quick hug, holding on for a second or two longer than 'friends' probably should and then she invited me inside.

"It's good to see you. I don't know about you, but I am so hungry. I haven't eaten since this morning. My dad won't be a second; he's just finishing up on a work call."

She playfully squeezed my hand as she led me through to the kitchen/dining area. I was in awe of how beautiful the inside of the house was. It was obvious that a considerable amount of thought and effort had gone into making everything as perfect as it was.

"No problem. This place is beautiful. Who designed all this, your mum?"

"Yes, she did with a bit of help from my dad. It was her project when we moved here because she wanted something to occupy her mind. I guess it's nice because, in a way, we are constantly reminded of her. She meticulously thought out every part of the house, so it's nice to have those memories of her everywhere we look. She designed it to be timeless, hoping that she wouldn't have to change anything for a really long time. Everything is exactly how she left it, apart from these pictures we hung on the wall after she passed."

She pointed to the many portraits of her mum and the rest of the family. There were over 40 photos, a picture for every year of her life, it seemed, starting from baby photos all the way up to what must have been the last family photo of them all. Her mum looked so young, so beautiful. I wondered how long after the photo she passed, but I didn't want to comment too much. I knew it would be a tough subject.

"The photos are great. Your mum was really beautiful. I see where you get it from now."

She smiled shyly and continued into the kitchen where her father had just entered through the large, sliding doors from the garden.

"Hi, you must be Holly. Nice to meet you."

He extended his hand to shake mine. Very formal, I should've predicted that.

"Mr Jacobs, it's lovely to meet you too."

"Please, call me Robert. Brooke has told me a lot about you. I'm glad she's got a good friend to look out for her; some of her friends have been rather questionable in the past."

A good friend, if only he knew I wanted to be so much more than that. I smiled politely and tried not to seem so intimidated, which proved difficult. Brooke's father had a certain aura about him, a presence that made you question whether or not you'd already gotten on his bad side.

"Dad, my friends aren't that bad! He believes the majority are immature and don't respect themselves. I agree slightly with the second statement, but they're good girls."

Robert rolled his eyes before turning his attention back to me.

"So, what are you both doing today?"

"Just going for some food and a catch-up, I think."

I looked towards Brooke for some reassurance that was still the plan and she nodded.

"So, you're a lawyer, Holly? That must be a tough gig. How long have you been qualified?"

Just like that, the subject had changed and I suddenly felt as though I was under immense pressure to provide intelligent answers.

"Yes, I am. It will be six years now since I joined West & Barnes. It's challenging and every case is completely different, so it's certainly interesting. I enjoy it; the long hours and the caseloads aren't for everyone, but it was something I always aspired to be, so it just came naturally to me, I suppose."

He watched me intently as I spoke. I wasn't sure if he was trying to put me under pressure, but it was something I had grown familiar with in my job, so I kept my composure.

"Good, life's too short to do something you despise. I have worked closely with some lawyers in my time and I admire the craft, the amount of work that goes into what you do. Brooke has told me she enjoys working there as well, so it must be a good atmosphere. Anyway, I'll let you get on. Make sure you're back in good time, Brooke. The family will want to see you."

He smiled politely towards me before kissing his daughter on the cheek and heading to the lounge.

"Shall we go?"

I nodded and followed her towards the front door.

"It was nice to meet you, Robert, have a good evening," I called after him as he walked away.

"You too, Holly, take care."

We climbed into the car and headed for The Fairview Inn.

"Well, I think that went pretty well, don't you? Your dad doesn't seem too bad, although he does have quite a presence about him, and I have dealt with some *overwhelming* people in my career."

She laughed at my emphasis on the word overwhelming.

"I agree, he doesn't normally want to have a 'quick' chat with my friends, though, which is strange, but I'm sure I will find out exactly what he thinks when I get home. He can be quite intimidating and, unless you're family or close friends, you don't really see the fun, happy-go-lucky Robert Jacobs."

She smiled.

"Maybe I'll get to see that side of him one day; who knows."

"Who knows." She winked.

The conversation flowed as easily as ever. We spoke about movies, hobbies, work, the usual type of thing. After the food, she slipped her hand across the table to hold mine. She was hesitant at first, but she soon forgot about the people around her and just embraced the romantic connection that was so evidently clear.

There was never any pressure, from my point of view. I knew it was something new for her; I knew she would take things at her own pace, which didn't bother me in the slightest. I could feel the connection we had growing stronger with every touch, every kiss, every phone call that lasted until the early hours of the morning. What we had was unique, and I hoped that she felt as strongly as I did.

We laughed and joked all the way back to her house. I had to make sure she was back in time for her family gathering and the last thing I wanted to do was upset Mr Jacobs, so there was an element of clock watching.

She asked me to pull over around the corner from her house, so I did.

"I can take you to your door, you know? Are you hiding me from your family?"

I laughed awkwardly, hoping that wasn't the case.

"No, silly, I wanted to make sure I could do this."

I heard the sound of the seatbelt unclip and she leant across. She placed one hand on the left side of my face and pulled my lips towards hers. Her lips brushed across mine so lightly at first that it sent shivers down my spine. As the kiss grew deeper, I pulled at her waist, hoping she could somehow get closer. She climbed across the seat to sit delicately in my lap, both hands now caressing my neck and running through my hair whilst I gripped the outside of her thighs. The desire burning inside was unbearable and never had a kiss felt so right. Her tongue brushed the inside of my mouth, occasionally pulling out and biting my bottom lip as she retracted.

Before we could get carried away, the buzz of Brooke's phone brought an end to the moment and threw us right back into reality.

"Shit, it's my dad. I better go. I'm already 20 minutes late. I loved tonight, as always. Being with you is…" she paused as if trying to find the right word, "…perfection."

"I'm just sorry it couldn't have been longer. Text me later?"

It was a silly question because I knew she would, at the first opportunity she got.

"Of course. See you tomorrow at the office."

She gave me another quick peck before jumping out of the car and slowly jogging out of sight. I wondered, at that moment, how long it would be until I could exclusively spend time with her as more than just friends. There was a feeling in the pit of my stomach that told me it might be a while. By the time I got home and got into bed, I was ready to relax and watch a movie.

There was a text from Brooke that left me with a feeling of utter disbelief.

The message read:

I can't see you anymore. My dad said there is something not right about our 'friendship'. He told me I need to stop whatever it is we are doing. I told him it wasn't like that and we are just friends, but he won't believe me. I started to get upset, so I'm currently sat in my room, trying to pull myself together. I don't want to make this any harder than it already is. I am so sorry.

I was speechless. For the first time in my life, I was actually speechless. It felt like a heavyweight blow. I hadn't put much emphasis on what was happening with us but I did think it was at least heading in the right direction. Now I had to come to terms with the realisation that it might not even get off the ground. My reply was instantaneous, so many questions running through my mind.

Why on earth would he think this is more than a friendship? I only met him once. How can he draw that conclusion from 5 minutes? I don't understand.

The typing bubble popped up immediately, and I waited anxiously for her reply.

The way we looked at each other, apparently. He said he had suspicions because of how much we talk and how distracted I am 24/7 when I'm talking to you. I also think my brother has been making sly comments to try and stir the situation, as always. So, he wanted to see how we acted in person and his words were, 'you look at her like a puppy dog looks at its owner for attention'. Yeah, odd, I know! He followed on to say it 'wasn't fair' for me to lead you on; therefore, he doesn't want me to see or talk to you anymore. I was so frustrated, so I just told him the whole thing is ridiculous and stormed off.

Was it that obvious to see there was something more between us? It's hard to know when you're in the situation, but even I have seen my friends like someone before they even admit it themselves. Parents can often pick up on those things and we had clearly underestimated him.

So, basically, what you're saying is your dad is homophobic? He's denying his daughter the chance to be happy?

I was becoming more and more infuriated. I had never understood homophobia. Why do people feel the need to try and deny someone happiness just because they disagree with it? It highlighted all that was wrong with the world. My family had always been so accepting of my sexuality, and it didn't matter to them whether I fancied men or women. I loved that about them, but unfortunately, many people didn't have the same luxury.

I know this isn't easy. He has never come across as homophobic, and I don't believe he is so it's hard to explain. I have never been with a woman before, so if he thinks that's what is happening, that is understandably going to be a shock for him. I don't know what to say right now. Obviously, I don't want to stop seeing you; that is the last thing I want. I am crying my eyes out at the thought of never seeing you, never kissing you, never talking to you. That's not something I can just let go of. I think he's just being dramatic. I have denied that we are anything more than friends, so maybe it will blow over.

What concerned me was the ease with which she denied having anything to do with me. I understood that what we had was in the early stages: We hadn't put a label on anything, we hadn't said I love you, we hadn't even had sex, but the connection we had was undeniable. The electricity that coursed through my veins every time we kissed, or I felt her hand touch mine was terrifying. The intensity when our eyes locked and our conversations flowed was unlike anything I had ever experienced.

Was it crazy of me to want her to turn around to her dad and say she wanted to be with me? Was it unreasonable to think that she might risk her dad being disappointed in her to have the chance of being with me?

The conversation went around in circles for the rest of the night. I think I was hoping to get answers that she wasn't going to give, looking for some form of reassurance, but she couldn't give me that. As much as she might have wanted to, the fact was, she couldn't. She didn't know how her father might react in the future, and she didn't know if he would ever accept the idea that she might be more than friends with a girl.

My head was throbbing by the time midnight struck. It was time for bed, time to let my dreams take me to a place where there were no complications, where me and Brooke lived happily ever after in a world without discrimination. My final thought echoing in my head *'would it always just be a dream?'*

CHAPTER FOURTEEN

"My dad is away tonight with work, and my brother is at his girlfriend's, which means I have the house all to myself. How would you feel about coming over after work?"

The invitation was a no brainer.

"I would love to come over but isn't that a bit risky? What if your Dad was to come home?"

She paused on the line for a second.

"I very much doubt he will, and I'm willing to take that risk. I need to be with you; I can't wait any longer."

That was good enough for me.

"I'll be over as soon as I'm done."

It was December 29th, Christmas had been and gone, the Boxing Day sales were well underway and people had already begun to take their Christmas decorations down, another year done. There was no change in the situation with Brooke and I. We hadn't stopped talking, quite the opposite, actually. After the initial shock of her father pretty much dooming her to a life of misery, we had decided that dwelling on it wouldn't make it any easier. I couldn't stop talking to her. I couldn't even stop thinking about her for more than a minute.

Things just became more challenging as we decided to do everything in secret. She had changed my name in her phone, so her father wouldn't see my name popping up all the time, removed me from her screensaver (going back to a picture of her and her mum) and, to top it off, she had handed her notice in at work.

That came as a shock at first. I couldn't believe the lengths she was going to, but she didn't need the job; her dad could provide for her until she found another. I wasn't entirely surprised that he had expected her to do that. Apparently, she had put up a fight, pleading with him, arguing that she really enjoyed her job and the whole thing was getting out of hand. He wouldn't listen, just made some excuse about how she had needed to do it for a long time so she could figure out what she wanted to do with her life. I knew full well that was a lie, and I think she did too, but there was a part of her that was still trying to protect her dad so that he wasn't painted as such a bad guy.

More often than not, our conversations had ended up going down a sexual path, and every other message we sent contained a rude emoji, some form of sexual innuendo or, if I was lucky, a nude photo. My mobile phone was quickly filling up with her content, being as it was the only way we could see each other.

It had been two weeks since we'd first kissed and how time had flown. Some days, it felt like torture, not knowing when or if I would be able to see her. I clung to any contact I could get, but then I found myself feeling even worse afterwards.

I told myself to walk away, forget all about her, find someone that I didn't have to hide from the world but that was easier said than done. I was fixated; every little thing she did drew me closer. It was too late. I couldn't walk away, even if I wanted to.

All I could think about was getting to Brooke as fast as possible. I had to be careful not to break the speed limits as I drove out of London and towards her house. I had been so eager to spend as much time with her as possible that I'd left work an hour earlier than usual.

As I pulled up, I made sure to park my car out of sight, as per Brooke's instructions. Her father had cameras on the front of the house, so she'd instructed me to go around the back so that she could turn them off for a minute whilst I entered the house.

It was a stealth operation. I had to be careful that the neighbours didn't see me because one of them was a good friend of Robert's, and he would always look out for Brooke whenever Robert was away on business. Said neighbour prided himself on his job as the lookout, always calling round in the evening to check everything was okay before Brooke locked up for the night. The orders of an obsessively protective father, without a doubt.

Once I dodged the neighbour, the cameras and the outdoor light, I was on the home stretch. I could see Brooke stood in the doorway, eagerly waving me inside.

"Hurry, be quick, hurry!" she half-whispered, half-shouted.

One more step and I was in. The door slammed shut behind me and I was in the safety of her house.

"I'm glad you made it."

She was stood directly in front of me, her breath on my neck as she moved closer. She wore an oversized, white shirt that fell across her body in all the right places. She hadn't bothered to wear trousers, just a tiny, black thong that aroused me even more.

"So am I."

I whispered the words as my lips brushed against hers. My whole body trembled. She raised her right eyebrow suggestively, and that was enough to send me over the edge. I grabbed both her arms and pushed her back, flat up against the wall with her wrists above her head. The kisses were long and deep. I couldn't control the passion inside of me. She pushed her thigh up in between my legs while pulling my waist in towards her. I had never felt a desire like it.

She pulled away from my mouth and moved towards my neck, working her way up to my ear where she delicately whispered, "Bedroom, please."

It may sound cliché when people say my heart skipped a beat, but I knew, at that moment, what that felt like. She wanted me as desperately as I wanted her; that was evident in the way she spoke so softly yet with so much conviction. She pulled me towards the stairs and we climbed up, step by step, without our lips parting once. It seemed to take forever to reach the top of the stairs; it didn't help that she lived in a house with a sweeping staircase and way more steps than necessary.

Once we reached the top step, I didn't have time to take anything in as she pulled me straight towards the bedroom down the hall on the right and, just like that, the door was locked behind me, and my belt was already being undone. I pulled my hoodie over my head and proceeded to unbutton her shirt. She sat on the edge of the bed, pulling my waist towards her. She unbuttoned my jeans and looked up towards me for reassurance. I cupped her face with my hands, bending down to kiss her lips again and again.

"Are you sure? It's okay to be nervous; I am."

She looked me straight in the eye and answered without hesitation in her voice.

"I have never been so sure of anything."

She lay back on the bed in nothing but the thong, leaving very little to the imagination. I was grinning from ear to ear as I climbed onto the bed and pushed my body up against hers. Our bodies fit together so naturally; her skin was soft, her lips were just the right size to compliment mine. Everything just felt right. I kissed every inch of her body, taking it all in as I worked my way down towards her thong, slowly slipping it off one leg. She used her foot to push my jeans down my legs as I came back up towards her mouth.

"If I'm naked, you're naked."

I smirked and ran my hand up the inside of her leg, teasing over and over again. I felt her nails dig into my back as my fingers eventually slipped inside her. Her moans were addictive as they grew louder and louder until she finally reached a climax.

There was sweat dripping off the both of us as I lay beside her, exhausted but far from done.

The next few hours were a blur. She had tried several times to please me but failed. It wasn't easy, so I didn't expect anything more but, for someone's first time with a woman, she had exceeded all of my expectations.

"I am sorry I couldn't... you know. I feel bad. Are you disappointed?"

We lay side by side now, looking into each other's eyes.

"No, don't be silly. Just being able to be here, with you and do this, is incredible."

She smiled and softly kissed me once again.

"It's just so different."

"What is?"

"Being with a woman, it's just better. I feel like everyone should experience this."

I laughed out loud, trying to wipe the smirk from my face. I guess you could say that I was rather pleased with myself.

"Oh? Well, I'm glad you enjoyed yourself."

"I did. It just feels right."

There was a pause as if she wanted to say something else.

"What?"

"I just wish we didn't have to do all the sneaking around, you know? I can't explain to you how right this feels, how easy it is. It's like I have known you my whole life. I wasn't even scared to do this, and this is a hell of a big deal to me. You've done this before, I haven't, and I just feel so happy in your presence, like I would try anything and go anywhere with you. Is that weird?"

She flipped onto her back and stared up at the ceiling. I got the sense she had said too much. She looked vulnerable, but there was no need to be.

"No, that's not weird at all. I wish we didn't have to sneak around too, but I know this is hard for you and I'll wait as long as I need to. Hopefully, one day, you'll be able to do anything with me and go anywhere."

I propped myself up on my elbow and leaned over to kiss her.

"I hope so."

My alarm rang out. I was in a state of confusion; was I at work today? I could've sworn it was my day off. I turned over to find my phone, but my phone wasn't there. Instead, there was Brooke, and it was Brooke's alarm going off.

"Brooke, wake up. What time is it? We must have fallen asleep."

She sat upright and immediately turned to grab her phone.

"Shit, shit, shit, how did we fall asleep? My brother will be back any minute."

Just like clockwork, we heard the latch downstairs open.

"He will be calling in to get his football stuff. I knew he wouldn't have taken them to Lucy's; he never does. You need to hide, quick. Go in the bathroom."

I grabbed my hoodie and jeans from the floor and ran to the en-suite across the other side of the bedroom.

"Brooke, it's only me. Have you seen my football boots?" her brother shouted out.

I could hear him bounding up the stairs, on a mission to find them.

"Don't come in my room. I'm not dressed, and no, I haven't seen them, sorry. Check the garage; that's where dad's probably chucked them if you left them lying around the kitchen again."

I heard his footsteps stop just outside Brooke's door; his voice came through clearly from the other side.

"Thanks, sis, I'll look there. See you in a bit. Say 'Hi' to your friend for me."

He bolted back down the stairs as quickly as he had come up, laughing to himself.

"Shit, how does he know someone's here?"

I could see the panic on Brooke's face as she searched for her sweater.

"Maybe he's just bluffing. Even if he does know someone's here, he won't know it's me, so don't panic. You could have just invited one of your friends over to stay."

I stopped her in her tracks as she paced the room and pulled her close to me. I kissed her on the forehead, our height ratio, making it the perfect place to plant a quick kiss.

"Yeah, maybe you're right. My brother isn't stupid, though; he knows I would have told dad if I was having someone over. Oh God, maybe he's seen your shoes at the bottom of the stairs? This was such a risky idea. How could we have been so stupid to fall asleep."

I quickly grabbed the rest of my belongings from her dressing table and headed toward the bedroom door.

"I'm sorry that I've put you in this situation. There is nothing I can say or do that is going to make this any easier for you. Last night was exactly what I hoped it would be, but we have to return to reality. I'll see myself out."

I closed the door behind me and left as quickly and as stealthily as I had entered the night before.

On my drive home, it started to resonate how hard this was going to be. I tried not to dwell too much on the future, but it was hard to think of anything else when I could see it being taken away before it had even been fully explored. I think that's what made it harder, the unknown.

Was the special bond we had worth fighting for? Did we have the potential to be happy, to be a storybook kind of love? When you know you can't have something, they say that it makes you want it even more, and that was always at the back of my mind.

It was New Year's Eve, and I hadn't spoken to Brooke all morning, not since the night before when we had entered into another conversation that was only going to end one way. It was becoming a regular occurrence: We would talk about seeing each other, we'd talk about the possibility of being able to kiss one another, sleep side by side and lie in bed all day, all the things that any normal couple could do.

Except we weren't normal, and there was a big obstacle in our way that never seemed to budge. The conversation would get a little more heated, often becoming more serious than it probably needed to be, considering we weren't even in a relationship. We had spoken about 'labels' and what that meant for us, but it seemed ridiculous at the time to put a label on anything. Nobody would even know there was an 'us'.

We both agreed that we wouldn't date other people. I believed that she was the girl for me, which meant that the urge to speak to other people had become non-existent. I gave her the benefit of the doubt, trusted her in whatever capacity I could trust her, and I hoped, with all my being, that our situation might change. That was always the one thing I hoped, above everything else.

The conversation often got to the same point when there was nothing else to say. We knew what position we were in, and though I tried not to blame her for essentially keeping me a secret, there was nobody else I could blame when it came down to it.

I picked up the phone and called her just after lunchtime. I didn't want there to be any hostility between us. After a brief greeting on both parts, we quickly forgot about the night before.

"Are you still free tonight?" Brooke asked.

"It's New Year's Eve and, as much as I would like to say I have plans, unfortunately, I do not."

My New Year's plans had undoubtedly taken a turn for the worse. I usually attended a friend's house party, but most of my friends had sided with Danielle after the break-up, which meant my options had become somewhat limited.

There was nothing that excited me more than the possibility of seeing Brooke. The chances were very slim, but in all honesty, the speck of hope was the only thing that kept me going. The hope that the situation might change. I quickly came to realise that humans are a sucker for two things: Love and hope.

"My dad thinks I'm staying at Amy's. I was hoping maybe I could detour and stay at yours instead? I don't know what I'll say to Amy, I haven't figured that bit out yet, but there's only one person I'd want to see the New Year in with."

I couldn't contain my grin on the other end of the phone. Maybe my evening was going to become a lot more desirable after all.

"I would love that. My evening was going to consist of a few beers and a takeaway for one, but I wouldn't say no to some company. What time are you thinking of coming over?"

It was one of those occasions where I was happy the conversation wasn't in person because the smile on my face was uncontainable, and it made me feel somewhat embarrassed.

"I'll figure out the timings later on, but I'd love nothing more than to be with you tonight. I'm heading over to Amy's at 6 to get ready. I'm hoping I can get Amy drunk enough by midnight so that as soon as we see the New Year in, I can send her home in a taxi and make my way to your house."

"That sounds like a plan; I'll look forward to it. Keep me posted."

"Me too. I'll text you later. Love ya."

"Speak later. Bye."

The L-word had started to appear in recent days; whether it was by phone or text, it was used freely in a friendly manner. Brooke had been the first to say it on a phone call and we both acknowledged it had been said but not in the way I one day hoped it would be.

I had known Brooke for three months; we had spoken almost every day. We built a bond, a friendship, even a bit more, and I knew nearly everything about her. It only made me love her more. We subconsciously tried to make the wording casual to not confuse it with actually telling each other we loved each other, a milestone I felt I would hit sooner rather than later.

Like anyone, I think I wanted that moment to be special. I didn't want to say it too soon or at the wrong moment and, most importantly, if I didn't mean it. When you tell someone that you love them, to me, you are opening your heart to that person, allowing them in, and the vulnerability that comes with those words is heightened.

I always struggled with how long to leave it before telling someone that I loved them. Can a time frame be put on a decision like that? Everybody is different; people have said it after three days, three weeks, three months.

I had known Brooke for almost three months, we had grown significantly closer towards the latter end, and if I was completely honest with myself, I had never felt the way I felt about Brooke for anyone else, not even Danielle. I did wonder if it was lust as I was newly single, which meant it could very well be a distraction.

Did I love Brooke? That was a question I was trying to put off for as long as possible.

It was 7:30 pm on New Year's Eve. I had just ordered myself a Chinese takeaway and I was about to see what Netflix had to offer. I felt the need to play a movie relevant to the night, so I chose 'New Year's Eve', starring a host of big Hollywood names. I had seen it once before and enjoyed its easy-going feel-good factor.

My phone buzzed as I sat down to eat. Brooke's message was a picture of her outfit and the caption simply read 'Do you approve?'.

'WOW' was all that came to mind. She looked out of this world. Her hair was long and curled effortlessly around the front of her body. She had a tight, black dress that accentuated every curve. Her legs looked long and tanned, a killer combination; the nude heels she wore complimented them perfectly. I stared at the photo for a good five minutes before I remembered I needed to reply.

You look incredible. Like, seriously unbelievable.

Her reply was almost instant.

Thank you, baby. I'm all yours.

The grin on my face had become uncontrollable; the instant feeling of overwhelming happiness was hard to contain. I was thankful not to be in the company of anyone else at that point; the thought of someone witnessing my child-like excitement was mortifying.

I liked the use of 'baby'. She had started to call me by that term in recent weeks, and it filled me with a sense of pride, making me feel as though I was hers and she was mine. After all, she did say 'I'm all yours' and I felt like she was. Well, as much as she could be.

I love it when you call me 'baby'. I am one lucky girl to have you in my life. I can't wait to see you later.

I meant every word I said to her. The more we spoke, the deeper the affection became, and the more our messages to one another started to take a meaningful turn. It wasn't harmless flirting anymore; it was so much more than that and we were both slowly coming to that realisation.

I can't wait to see you too like you wouldn't believe. I am the lucky one. Meeting you was the best thing that ever happened to me and I genuinely mean that.

My heart skipped a beat every time I received a message like that, it reaffirmed in my head the way she felt about me and it made me realise that it wouldn't all be for nothing. Brooke was the person I wanted to be with, that was one thing

I was sure of, and I would continue to fight for that until she alone told me not to.

I didn't speak to her much for the rest of the night, I didn't want her to be distracted by me whilst she was out with her friends. She sent a text every half hour or so to check in and I was well aware of what she was doing through various social media platforms.

As it grew closer to midnight, I became more and more excited at the prospect of seeing her. I had quickly been upstairs to freshen up, conscious that she would be all dressed up, and I had been lying around for most of the night. The clock ticked just past midnight and I received a FaceTime call from Brooke. She was outside her local pub, I could hear the fireworks exploding behind her, but all I could focus on was the face that I had missed so much.

"Hey, you."

"Hey, beautiful." I replied.

She smiled her ever-so-perfect smile before responding.

"I can't hear you very well so I'll make it quick, but I just wanted to say Happy New Year and…" There was a slight pause on the line before she said the next part. "I love you."

She wasn't laughing; she wasn't smirking; she was deadly serious. She loved me.

"You love me?"

She didn't shy away from the question. Maybe it was the liquid courage, though she didn't seem overly intoxicated, but feelings were always intensified when alcohol was involved. She sensed the uncertainty in my voice, but that only made her more eager to relay her feelings.

"I love you; surely, you know that. I have wanted to say it for weeks. To be honest, I just wasn't sure if you felt the same. I'm sat here when all I want to do is be there with you. I'm drinking and dancing and getting this attention from people, but all I can think about is you. You have just taken over my head. I was thinking to myself earlier, 'how do I know if I love her' and then it was like a light bulb moment."

There was a brief pause on the line as if she was trying to collect her thoughts before continuing.

"You're the first thing I think about every morning, the only person I hope to see a text from when I look at my phone. There is barely a minute that goes by that my mind isn't overrun with thoughts of you. When I think about my future, I only see you, so I think it's pretty obvious. I do love you, and it's the hardest thing I have ever had to do, keep the one I love a secret from my friends and family, but I promise you that it will be different one day. One day, we will be together on New Year's Eve, with your family and with my family, bringing the New Year in together. I know I'm rambling on and potentially scaring you off because you haven't even said it back."

Brooke immediately stopped talking and looked around for witnesses, realising she had just poured her heart out on a FaceTime call in front of a bunch of drunken strangers.

The signal wasn't the best, but I made out almost every word she said, minus a few vowels. I could see the fear on her face, that moment of dread when you are wondering if your feelings will be reciprocated or shot down. It might not have been the most romantic way of expressing her love, but it was a modern era and technology always seemed to be incorporated into significant moments.

My smile said a thousand words before I even had a chance to respond.

"I love you too. I know that with absolute certainty. It probably isn't how I would have told you, but Brooke Jacobs, you are the most random and perfect person I think I have ever met. I really hope we can experience New Year's the way you have described it. That would be a dream come true."

The signal started to break slightly and I was struggling to hear what she said next. I could see Amy's face come into view; it looked like she had been crying. Brooke quickly said goodbye and the call ended. I was sure I'd hear all about whatever drama Amy had gotten herself into later that night.

The time was 12:45 am, so I climbed into bed and awaited a response from Brooke. She hadn't replied since she left the FaceTime call just after midnight, but I assumed that she was comforting her friend, making me wonder whether I would get to see her at all.

Eventually, my phone started to ring and Brooke's name flashed on the screen.

"Baby, I have some bad news."

I think I already knew what was coming before the words left her mouth.

"You can't come over? I'm guessing some drama with Amy?"

I hit the nail on the head.

"I'm sorry. She rang her boyfriend at midnight, and he basically told her he didn't want to be with her anymore. The timing is horrendous. When I have sobered up tomorrow, I'll be having words with him, but I'm just sorry that I can't come over. As you can imagine, I can't leave her in the state she's in. She's had a hell of a lot to drink, and everything is heightened right now, so of course, she feels like her world is going to end."

Although it was disappointing, I did understand and I would have done the same for one of my friends. She had a moral obligation to stay with her, make sure she was okay, and I respected that. I tried to hide the disappointment in my response.

"I understand. I'm gutted, but I get it, so don't worry. You need to do right by your friend. Her boyfriend sounds like a piece of work."

I didn't know anything about Amy's boyfriend and I didn't have any right to comment, but I felt the need to side with Brooke. After all, no matter what may have happened, it's a bit of a crappy thing to do, breaking up with your partner at midnight on New Year's Eve.

"Thank you for being so understanding. I meant what I said earlier, I love you, and there will be next New Years. Speak to you tomorrow."

I should have been excited at the prospect of the following New Year's but, instead, I felt a lump in my throat. The uncertainty was overruling any excitement I should have been feeling. I pushed it away (as I did most days) and just hoped for the best.

"I love you too. Sleep well."

The sun was piercing through my dark grey curtains - My first thought, *'I should have bought the blackout ones'*. I went for the fancier version and my punishment was being woken up most mornings; it was time to purchase a new set.

New Year's Day, what a lovely day to start 2019. It was chilly outside - as you would imagine for that time of year - but the clear, blue skies and the sun beating down would've been deceptive enough to trick anyone into thinking it was summer. It was 10 am, a decent lie-in by most people's estimations, but I hadn't gotten to sleep until around 2 am. I could've easily had a few more hours.

I had a phone call from my mum and dad, wishing me a 'Happy New Year' followed quickly by a phone call from Paula, telling me about her wild night out, which she was now fiercely regretting. I headed downstairs to make a cup of coffee and some scrambled egg on toast for breakfast. It wasn't the most exotic food choice, but it was quick and straightforward, and that's how I liked things.

Over an hour passed by after breakfast, and my phone started to ring again. It was Beth. Beth was my oldest friend; she had moved away to Tokyo to teach English almost four years prior. We had been inseparable up until the age of 22, so seeing her leave was heart breaking. It had meant I had the opportunity to explore Tokyo on three occasions whilst she had been out there, so there was always a silver lining.

We made a pact always to visit each other at least once a year. She would, more often than not, come home two or three times due to school holidays, so I got to see her more than we'd agreed, which was a welcome surprise. We didn't get to talk much (due to the time difference), but it was always as if nothing had changed when we got back together.

Beth had met her boyfriend in Tokyo in her third year there. They had been together for two years. She had decided to stay with him and his family for Christmas. She felt it was only fair as he had come over the year before to meet her family. So, instead, she was coming back in the New Year. There had been some delays with flights which meant she didn't get in until early New Year's Day, but I was beyond excited to see her and I knew, as soon as that picture flashed up on my phone, that my day was about to get a whole lot better.

"B…"

"H…"

Her real name was Bethany; her nickname was Beth and, to me, she was B. She had taken it upon herself to call me H, so together, we were B and H.

"Honestly, you have no idea how excited I am to hear your voice. Please tell me you have landed on British soil?"

"I certainly have, safe and sound. I can't wait to see my best friend. The family can wait; I need to see you first! Fancy meeting me at our favourite spot? It's been a while."

Our favourite spot was Nina's Café. We had been going there for years. Nina's was famous for some of the best pancakes in London. Not only that, but they also made the most incredible coffee with latte art that was out of this world. Every time we went, I tried to challenge them, and they always delivered. Most people would ask for a heart or a star, but, on my last coffee, I had opted for a Buddha and it was insane.

"It has been a while, too long. Sounds like a plan. I'm sure we have a lot of catching up to do! Is Ren with you?"

The last time Beth was in the UK, Nina's was being refurbished, so it had been roughly a year since we had last been. I was having withdrawals.

"I have so much to tell you. I have, no word of a lie, been making notes on my phone because I just knew I would forget most of it. No, Ren has to work over New Year, so I'm flying solo."

Ren was Beth's boyfriend. From what I had seen of him, he was a good guy; he was kind to her and treated her like a princess, surprising her with gifts and trips. He was easy on the eye as well, probably one of the most handsome men in Tokyo.

"I can't wait to hear all about it! When will you be there?"

I could hear the trains calling out on the platform in the background.

"I'm waiting for the train now. I should be about 30 minutes, I think."

I bounded up the stairs to get ready.

"Don't give me any time to get ready, will you? You're a nightmare. I can be ready in 20, so you'll just have to sit tight. Probably take me 20 minutes to get there on the underground.

I'll let you know when I'm 5 minutes away so you can get the drinks in!"

"Hurry up; I know what you're like. See you soon."

I walked into Nina's 42 minutes after that phone call ended and there was Beth, all big-eyed and beautiful. She was certainly a thing of beauty. To tell the truth, when I first met Beth, I found her beauty undeniable. We hit it off instantly and became the best of friends, but there was a time when I wished, more than anything, that she wasn't as straight as she was.

Beth had always turned heads. She stood at 5'11". Her hair was a very light brown and naturally curly. She had the most piercing, blue eyes, a button nose and plump lips. She had grown into her thin, lanky frame over the years, and she now stood a tall, curvy woman with a body that most would envy.

Beth leapt from her chair as I entered, and I saw her eyes light up, her grin beaming from ear to ear. Nothing made me happier than seeing that face. Well, almost nothing.

She bellowed across the café, despite the many customers in between us.

"Holly Garland, get over here right now and give me a cuddle."

I laughed at her overzealous greeting. She was the most confident person I knew; she didn't care what other people thought about her. I fought my way through the last few people between us and embraced her for what felt like the first time in forever.

"B, I have missed you, girl. It's so good to see you, and what are you wearing because you smell incredible?"

Beth always smelt good; it was her thing. When she was studying to be a teacher, she had worked part-time on a perfume stall so she could pretty much identify any perfume on the market. She was the reason I had so many bottles in my wardrobe, having bombarded me over the years. She felt that the most important thing was to smell good.

"I have missed you. It's Chanel, sweetie, and thank you. You smell good, is that last year's Christmas present I smell?"

She knew 100% that it was.

"It certainly is. You always keep me smelling good."

"Of course, I wouldn't have it any other way. You look good, H. You look happy."

She was always so sweet.

"Thank you, so do you, but I'm seeing my best friend and that always makes me happy."

She pushed my coffee towards me.

"Ditto. I got your favourite. There's just something about this place. Mike behind the counter greeted me as if I come here every day. I love how they remember us; it's so cute."

That was the spirit of Nina's. It was a small, family-run café and they almost always remembered customers by name. In a big, bustling city like London, that was a hard thing to do with the number of people that pass through on a daily basis.

"I know I love this place. So, how are you anyway? How was the flight?"

Beth took a sip of her coffee before diving straight in.

"The flight was good, always a long one, but I managed to upgrade when I got to the airport, so I had a comfier seat. I always have a million things to do on the laptop, so it went pretty fast."

She took another sip of her coffee which gave me enough time to reply.

"Good, I'm glad."

"How am I? Perfect, actually. You know me. Me and Ren are great; school is great. I feel like I make a difference out there, you know? I thought it might get old, but it hasn't yet, and I'm four years in, so I can't complain. Tokyo is amazing.

I'm still trying to see as much of Japan as I can. Whenever I get time off, me and Ren will go to someplace new. He's usually already been himself, but he always makes me feel like we are experiencing it together for the first time, which is nice. Oh, God, I didn't tell you."

Nothing good ever started with 'Oh, God'.

"Oh, no, what's happened?"

She was pulling her mortified face.

"A couple of weeks ago. I thought I was pregnant. Yes, pregnant. I just felt so nauseous, and I was really craving sushi, like, all the time and I don't even like sushi that much. I just didn't feel right and I was so worried. I mean, I am so not ready to have a child. I teach them all day long and that continuously puts me off. I told Ren and he freaked out, said he wasn't ready for kids and we got into a massive argument. Anyway, long story short, I did a pregnancy test and found out I wasn't pregnant, so the argument and the worrying was for nothing. If I have learnt one thing, it's that we are not ready for kids and, next time, do a test before making a massive deal out of it."

And breathe.

"Oh, okay, that's a new one. FYI though, I think you'd make a really good mum and, more importantly, I think I would like to be Auntie H one day. You would have to move back to the UK because I can't deal with not seeing my niece or nephew all the time."

Beth laughed out loud.

"FYI, you'll be waiting a while for that, and also, I love how you want me to move back to the UK when I have a baby and not before. Charming."

I took another sip of my coffee and smirked behind the mug.

"Let's be honest. You're not as cute as a baby; there's just not as much appeal there. I hate to break it to you."

She playfully smacked my hand from across the table.

"You're nasty! Anyway, apart from that, I'm all good. What about you? The last time I spoke to you on the phone, you were very shady about your recent whereabouts, and you know I can sense these things, so are you going to spill the beans? Or do I have to coerce it out of you?"

Over the past couple of months, I hadn't mentioned Brooke in any of our conversations. I wasn't sure why because if I could tell anyone anything, it would be Beth. I suppose a part of me didn't want her to judge the situation. Beth was very supportive of me and what I chose to do, but she was also very honest, and it wasn't always the kind of honesty you wanted to hear. As a best friend, she always felt the need to say it because if she couldn't, who else would.

If I was really honest with myself, I think I was embarrassed about being someone's secret. I had nothing to hide, and that was the hard part for me.

"What do you mean 'shady'? I had nothing to hide. Maybe you just didn't ask the right questions."

She looked surprisingly offended.

"You better tell me what's going on right now, Holly Garland."

The young woman on the table next to us glanced over, probably anticipating a full-blown domestic. I couldn't help but laugh.

"Okay, so there may have been something happening with someone from work for a couple of months now."

I could tell by her face that she was ready to hit me again.

"What am I supposed to do with that? You couldn't be any vaguer right now, but you have sparked my interest so, please, continue."

"It's a weird one. I don't know where to start."

My phone lit up at that moment; I glanced down to see a message from Brooke. I must have automatically smiled because Beth jumped for my phone and looked at the name on the front screen.

"So, her name's 'Brooke' then. Let me just go onto Instagram and have a look at anyone you follow with the name 'Brooke'."

She smirked, knowing she had caught me out. I knew that she'd find Brooke's profile in less than ten seconds.

"Brooke Jacobs. You could have made it harder for me, H. I mean, she's beautiful, really beautiful. Looks a little straight though, is she straight?"

Beth was hardly ever wrong; it was just a gift of hers. Her intuition had always been her superpower.

"People are only straight until proven otherwise."

She laughed.

"Hmmm, okay. So do you want me to keep digging, or do you just want to tell me what's happening?"

I looked at my coffee, almost all gone.

"We are going to need refills for this."

I headed to the counter and asked for the same again. Once I sat back down, Beth was poised and ready to hear the whole story, so I told her everything.

She was silent for about 30 seconds after I finished speaking, which was unheard of for her. I had explained our whole relationship, every encounter and read through a lot of text messages. Before we knew it, 40 minutes had passed and I don't think Beth had said more than two words.

"Why didn't you tell me this sooner? You've basically been having a relationship in secret for two months."

I sighed.

"I'm sorry, I wanted to tell you, I just didn't know how to. I didn't know where it would lead or if I would develop the feelings I have or if it would even work out. There is still a huge cloud of doubt over that, so it's hard. I felt a little embarrassed because I knew you would probably turn around and tell me I am worth so much more than to be kept somebody's secret."

She smiled and pulled my hand into hers.

"Let me tell you something. I love you, you're my best friend in the whole world, and I will always think you're worth so much more because you are, but there is a lot more context to this than even I can probably understand. You clearly love this girl and, from what you've shown me, she loves you too. The difficult part is deciding whether love is enough. We all fall in love, most of us do several times during the course of our lives, but sacrificing family and life as you know it for love is a burden that most aren't willing to carry."

Beth took a moment to gather her thoughts before continuing.

"Love shouldn't be hard, Holly, and it's not your fault that we are in a world where some people still can't accept sexuality. It's not your fault that this love you are experiencing now is harder than it should be, but it is your responsibility to decide whether it's worth it. You can't change her father's mentality. You can't change the life she currently finds herself leading, and ultimately, you can't change the decision she will eventually have to make. I will ask you this: If you have six months of this love and then you never see her again, will it be worth the heartache?"

I squeezed her hand. Why hadn't I told her sooner? She was always the voice of reason; she always knew exactly what to say and how to put things into perspective. I loved her for that. It was an easy response and there was absolutely no hesitation in my words.

"Right now, I would take a lifetime of heartache if it meant I could have another two weeks with her, let alone six months."

She smiled at me and squeezed my hand tighter.

"That's exactly the response I knew you would give. Do you know why?"

I shook my head.

"The way you spoke about her with such beaming pride, the way you carefully described all her greatest qualities and the look on your face every time you thought about the future and what that could hold for the both of you. You love her deeply; I can see that. It's embedded in everything that you say."

I was smiling from ear to ear. Beth was right; I did love Brooke more than I ever thought I could, which terrified me.

"Thank you for always being you. I don't know what I'd do without you."

CHAPTER FIFTEEN

The sunlight streamed through the blinds of my office window. It was nice to see some sun after the two weeks of continuous rain and snow we had just endured.

The date was January 23rd, me and Brooke had now been inseparable for three weeks. She had gotten rather good at telling white lies. As far as her father knew, she was either going to see a friend, going for a walk or going to the gym. He never really suspected much and I was thankful for every moment I got to spend with her. The more time I spent with her, the deeper my feelings became and I found myself wanting more; an hour here and there wouldn't suffice forever, and we both knew that.

There had been times when her brother's girlfriend, Lucy, had been invited to family meals and I wondered if that would ever be me. It was a hard pill to swallow, to know that Brooke was sat there, wishing I could be the one beside her, that I could be accepted into the family the same way Lucy was. It often turned into an argument and left me demanding whether or not she would ever pluck up the courage to finally tell her father about me.

I loved Brooke; I did not doubt that. We spoke about what trips we would take once we became official; the Maldives had been the first on the list, closely followed by Barcelona and then Thailand. We both liked a mixture of culture and sunshine on our holidays, so it was easy to agree on potential destinations. The thought of travelling with her one day filled me with joy like no other.

I had seen Brooke the day before when we had gone for a drive on the outskirts of London. We stopped off at a pub called The Inn, which had beautiful views of a National Park. She had told her father that she was going out with a friend she had recently reconnected with, Lewis. She had used Lewis on multiple occasions as an excuse for when she was coming to see me, and her father never seemed to bat an eyelid. I was growing considerably more curious as to why that would be.

"Does your dad think you're seeing Lewis? As in dating him? Because you have been seeing him a lot lately or so he thinks you have."

Her response was quick and standoffish.

"No, he thinks we are friends. I can have friends that are boys. It doesn't need to be more than that."

Just like clockwork, her phone started to ring; it was her father.

"Crap, crap, I don't want to answer it. What if he knows I'm not with Lewis? He never calls when I'm out. What am I supposed to say?"

I could sense the sheer panic straight away; her whole demeanour changed instantly.

"Just act normal. He's going to know something's wrong if you don't answer. Just play it cool."

There was a part of me that wanted her father to have figured it out, as horrible as that may seem. The longer it went on, the more I felt like she would never tell him. Prolonging the deceit only meant that he would need to find out some other way.

"Hi Dad, what's up?"

I tried to stay as silent as I could. Her father told her dinner would be at 6 pm sharp and if she wanted to invite Lewis, she could. My heart sank, knowing that her dad obviously thought there was something more between them and, even though there wasn't, he clearly wanted there to be.

"Okay, thank you, I'll be home soon. Bye, love you."

I could see the sadness engulf her face, and she could see the hurt in mine. Would it ever get easier? I often asked myself, genuinely searching for an answer.

"So, your dad wants Lewis to come round. What will you tell him when Lewis isn't there because you haven't actually been seeing Lewis?"

I saw a flash of guilt run across her face. That was something I hadn't seen before, a distinct look of unease, and I knew there was something she wasn't telling me. I felt inclined to probe a little deeper.

"You haven't seen Lewis, have you? Or is there something you're not telling me?"

She looked out of the window and then looked back at me, sighing deeply before she spoke.

"I did see him, but it's not like that. A few nights ago, when I told you I'd gone out with my friend Jenny, well…Lewis was there too. A group of us got together. I didn't tell you because I didn't see the relevance, but now my dad's making more of a deal out of it than it needs to be."

My heart sank into the pit of my stomach. That feeling of betrayal was one I instantly didn't want to become familiar with.

"Why would you hide that from me? If you had nothing to hide then you would have told me he was there with you."

She knew I had a point. I remembered asking her what she was doing, how her night was going, and she had every opportunity to mention that Lewis had also been there.

"Babe, I wasn't hiding anything from you; there was no relevance to Lewis being there. If I'd have told you, surely that would have seemed worse, like there was some reason I needed to tell you. There is no reason because nothing is going on, so I didn't tell you."

She grabbed my face with both hands and kissed me on the lips, looking directly into my eyes before she spoke again.

"I love you, Holly. There is nothing you need to worry about. I'm sorry, I didn't tell you. Lewis is a nice guy and someone I have known for a long time, but that's all. He's just a friend."

I wanted to believe her, but I had learned to trust my gut over the years, leading me to believe there was something not quite right. Maybe she just didn't see it herself.

"Okay, so what are you going to do? Are you inviting him over?"

She looked sheepishly at her phone.

"Not if I can avoid it. I'm going to talk to my dad when I get home and just tell him it's not like that with Lewis and me. It's too much pressure to put on me to ask him around for dinner. That should do the trick."

There was a small sigh of relief from me, and I felt my body relax back into the seat.

"Please just keep me in the loop. It's hard enough at the minute. I don't want to have a reason not to trust you as well."

She pulled me in for another kiss and the world around me just fell away. Those kisses were undeniable.

"I won't give you a reason not to trust me. I only want you, please, believe me."

How could I not believe her when she was kissing my lips and making her way down to my neck? I never wanted it to end.

"I only want you too. More than you'll ever know."

Brooke had managed to avoid inviting Lewis to dinner, but it was still playing on my mind the following day.

All of a sudden, I had a message from Brooke, then two, then three. My phone kept lighting up as they came in, one after the other, and I knew something wasn't right. I opened the stream of text messages, and they read as follows:

Holly, I am screwed.

My dad knows about you.

He knows I saw you yesterday.

Shit. What am I going to do?

HELP!!

I tried to call her immediately, but there was no answer. Another message came through.

He's pulling up in the drive now, can't talk. I need to put out this fire.

I quickly replied, in desperate need to know what was happening.

How did he know you were with me? I'm so confused.

She was typing instantly; the response took seconds.

His work friend saw me, asked him if I had a nice time at the Park and the conversation sparked from there. He knows I was with a girl, not a boy and now he knows I have lied to him, so he knows I'm trying to hide something. I'm going to have to do some damage control now. I'll ring you as soon as I can.

I didn't know how to respond. We had been quite reckless over the past month and the thought of someone seeing us, the word getting back to her father, hadn't crossed our mind. We tried to go as far away from the city as possible to be discrete, but that had now backfired.

For the rest of the afternoon, I did nothing but stare at my phone. An hour passed and then two with still no response from Brooke. A part of me thought maybe she had told him everything. Perhaps she had finally built up the courage to express how she felt and ultimately deal with the consequences. Maybe as I sat waiting, she was currently trying to bring him around to her way of thinking, explaining that she loved a girl and that wasn't a bad thing. Love was love, and it shouldn't matter whether it's with a man or a woman.

Just as I was starting to get concerned, I had a text message that would change everything.

That was painful, but I think I have managed to talk him around.

Does this mean he knows? Did she tell him the truth?

What have you told him?

I still held out hope.

I told him what I needed to. Yes, I was with you because you're my friend, and I should be allowed to see my friends. I shouldn't have to sneak around behind his back to see a friend at 24 years of age just because he is concerned it may be more than that. I told him that I wasn't gay. He was so angry for a minute. He told me that he would kick me out of the house if I didn't tell him the truth and if I didn't agree not to see you.

And just like that, all the hope was gone. That was her opportunity to tell him. He had caught her out, it was her chance to tell the truth, and she chose to sew the web of lies even more.

Oh, okay, so instead of taking the opportunity to tell him the truth, you chose to tell him you would never see me again. Did you even ask him what his problem was with me?

I could feel the hope being drained with every word I wrote.

I couldn't do it, Holl. You didn't see how angry he was. What would I do if he kicked me out? Where would I go? I have to think about things like that. This isn't some fairy tale where the bad guy eventually comes around to everyone else's way of thinking, and they all live happily ever after. Real-life isn't like that.

We all like to believe in fairy tales sometimes.

And what about me?

Brooke took a while to reply, and I could only assume she was trying to decipher the message she had gotten from her father, picking out the bits that wouldn't offend me too much.

Honestly... he said he knew I'd still been talking to you

because he's not stupid, but he thought it would fizzle out over time. What he didn't anticipate was your influence on me being as overbearing as it is. He said that this isn't my life, you're not good enough for me, and it's not the life he pictured for me. He said it was nothing personal towards you and that you're probably a really nice person, but you're not the person for his daughter, and you never will be.

The pain in my chest was overpowering. The tears streamed down my face as I quickly came to the realisation that the girl I loved would never really be my girl. I wondered if she even defended me, told him that I was a good person, that I would be perfect for her and I would give her the world if given the opportunity. I doubt any of that mattered to her father anyway; the deciding factor would always be my gender, which was the sad part. I could've been absolutely perfect for Brooke; I could've given her a life she dreamed of and made her the happiest she had ever been. None of that mattered. The hurt was made that much worse by Brooke's denial of us. If she loved me, wouldn't she have risked the world to be with me? I knew, if the shoe were on the other foot, I would have, in a heartbeat.

I was at a loss for words. It was almost time to leave the office, and I was thankful for the next two days off work. I needed the weekend to try to collect my thoughts. Brooke tried calling me twice on my journey home, but I didn't have the strength to talk to her. What I said didn't matter anymore if the outcome was always going to be the same.

When I finally got home, I had another text message.

Please talk to me. I'm sorry that my dad feels that way. I would give anything to change his opinion. Maybe we could just give him some time. Surely he will come around to the idea eventually. I'm sat here crying my eyes out because I don't want to lose you. I'm scared you're going to give up on me, and I don't know if I can cope with that.

How much time do you give a man like that?

Did I believe he would ever change his opinion? No, I didn't.

Did I believe Brooke would ever gain the courage to stand up to him and tell him I'm the one for her? No, I didn't, not anymore. So, where did that leave us?

I don't want to lose you, Brooke, that is the last thing I want, but we are running out of time. Whatever we have is running its course. It breaks my heart that you don't value me enough to stand up for me, to turn around to your dad and tell him that I'm the one for you. If I'm honest, that's probably what hurts the most.

The tears continued to pour; there was no stopping them now.

I am so sorry that I can't say what you want me to say, Holly. The thought of us ending is killing me inside right now. I have never felt pain like this since my mum passed away. I made a promise to her that I would look after my dad. I can't do the one thing that would tear this family apart. I hope you can at least understand that in some way.

That conversation felt like the end for us, and I wasn't so sure there was any way back.

CHAPTER SIXTEEN

It was a regular busy Friday at work, and I was thankful for the abundance of cases I had to deal with. It briefly took my mind of the one thing that never seemed to leave my mind: Brooke. A typical day varied so drastically that I didn't often have time to think about other things, but the past week had been tough. It had taken me to new lows; I couldn't eat, I couldn't sleep, I couldn't watch TV without my mind wandering to thoughts of Brooke.

We had both agreed that we would try to stop talking, that we would try our absolute best to distance ourselves so that it wouldn't be as difficult when the time came to sever all ties.

That had lasted about 12 hours.

We had finished our long, and heart-breaking conversation at around 2 am. Brooke messaged me the very next day at 2 pm. It was a simple gesture, asking if I was okay, if I had slept at all. A gesture that then led to a conversation that took us well into the evening. Neither of us could find it in ourselves to stop talking. Despite knowing the truth, despite all hope being lost, we couldn't let go.

The six days after that had been some of the hardest of my life. Every morning, I would wake up from minimal sleep, just for a second I wouldn't remember. It would fast come flooding back, and the knot in my stomach would return. Every night, I would dream of Brooke and a life that was far beyond my reach.

I had realised that letting her go would be the hardest thing I would ever have to do. It would take strength and courage I couldn't imagine possessing, but I knew that I would have to learn to build it, and that would take time.

We still spoke most days (that wasn't something either of us seemed to be able to cut off completely), but I hadn't seen her, and there was no plan to.

The conversations made me numb. We continued to go over and over the same scenarios, cry and fight, and wish that things could've been different more than ever.

I bombarded her with questions that I already knew the answers to. I asked her to change her mind. I asked her to give us a chance, just to find the courage to speak to her father. I told her that's all it would take for it to all work out, but my words fell short. The answers always came out the same, and the conversations only made me more upset.

The more we spoke, the harder it became to be apart because, without fail, we always fell back into our familiar ways of talking. We would act, for brief moments, as if nothing had changed, as if nothing was standing in our way of pure happiness. That was until we came back to reality, which we always did.

We spoke about trying to be friends, but the prospect was too hard at that moment in time. How could I bring myself to be friends with her, knowing what we had been through? How could I watch her be with someone else, knowing that she should have been with me?

My phone started to ring, and I was propelled out of the trance I had fallen into. It was Beth. She was due to go back to Tokyo in two days and that filled me with sadness. She had been my rock over the past week and had helped me come to terms with what I was facing.

"Hi, H, how are you feeling today?"

That familiar voice was always welcomed.

"Hey, B, I could be better, but I think it's clear I won't be myself for a while."

She paused, gathering her words.

"I know it's tough and what I'm about to tell you probably won't help matters, but I feel it's my duty, as your best friend, to tell you."

I instantly felt my heart sink.

"Oh. God. Go on, just tell me."

She hesitated.

"It's a weird story, but I didn't know that Tom Jacobs was Brooke's brother. I used to date him in college. I went shopping earlier and bumped into him. Anyway, we had a quick chat, and he told me that he'd seen I was living in Tokyo and asked me how it was because he might be moving to Japan in the next year to play football. I wasn't overly interested; you know I switch off when it comes to sports. Anyway, the conversation got onto Brooke; he asked if I remembered her, then it clicked."

Beth went quiet, letting the suspense build.

"Brooke Jacobs. I thought it couldn't have been a coincidence, and it turns out it wasn't. I said that my best friend Holly knows Brooke and what a small world it was. Basically, he knew who you were. He said, and I quote, *'is that the gay one that tried to seduce my sister?'* I laughed because he clearly didn't know the full story and God knows what crap his dad had been feeding him. He did take great pleasure in telling me this next part, though…"

A small world indeed. How had we not picked up on that sooner? How dare he put me down as some lesbian seductress?

That, I wasn't overly happy about. It sounded to me like he was just like his father.

"...so he told me *'he was glad Brooke had found a nice guy like Lewis and the family really liked him after getting together with him twice this week.'* Those were his exact words, Holly. The conversation ended very abruptly after that because, frankly, he had annoyed me, and I was about to slap him upside his head if I stayed any longer. I'm so sorry, I know this isn't what you want to hear right now, but I don't know what lies she's feeding you and you deserve the truth."

Betrayal was not just a hard pill to swallow; it was a shocking twist of a knife in my back. A deception that I didn't know if I could take at that moment in time.

"I don't know what to say; I appreciate you telling me. What do I do? I can feel myself shaking."

The tears started to stream, so I quickly closed the office door. I didn't want to be disturbed. I was surprised I had any tears left to cry. Just when I thought things couldn't get any worse, to learn that she had already started to move on was a low blow. How long had it been going on for? Had she been talking to him in that way before we even officially called things off? I guess there was only one way to find out.

"Just give yourself time to calm down. I know this will hurt, and I definitely think you should confront her, but you need to make sure it's at the right time. You have a right to know what's going on and how long it's been going on, especially with things between you two being so recent. I hope that Tom is wrong just so this doesn't become even more difficult for you."

I hoped he was wrong too.

"I will. I'll wait until I get home. I need some time to process this."

The line fell silent, a rarity for me and Beth.

"I love you, H. I'm sorry you're going through this. Just know it will get easier; it always does. Text me later, okay?"

That's what I used to tell people, *'it gets easier'*. If only I could've followed my own advice.

"Thanks, B. I love you too. I'll speak to you later."

The phone line went dead and I was left with a feeling of overwhelming sorrow. At that moment, I wasn't sure what was harder, knowing that Brooke wasn't willing to risk disappointing her father to be with me or knowing that it had taken her less than a week to move on. Both scenarios were unbelievably hard to grasp.

I had to wipe my tears, put on a brave face and finish the day's work when all I wanted to do was curl into a ball and never emerge.

The time ticked slowly past 5:30 pm and I couldn't do it anymore. The amount of work I had to do could've kept me there until the early hours of the morning. As a lawyer, there was a time when you simply had to call it a day. I had refrained from speaking to Brooke throughout the day. She had sent two text messages to which I hadn't replied. I couldn't hold a normal conversation knowing what I knew and I didn't want to broach the subject whilst being at work. I had no choice but to ignore the messages.

As soon as I walked through the door at home, I threw my bag down, kicked off my shoes and headed straight for the fridge. The thought of food, at that point, made me feel nauseous, but the idea of alcohol was more appealing and would maybe help soothe the pain. I composed close to 10 different messages, re-writing them repeatedly until I settled on the simplest of them all.

I'm going to ask you two questions and don't lie to me, Brooke.

I deserve more than that. Are you seeing Lewis? How long have you been seeing him?

Brooke's replies were typically instantaneous, but this one took a little longer. Fifteen minutes went by before I received the response I had been dreading.

I wondered why you had been ignoring my messages; now, it makes sense. I'm not seeing him, no, but I have seen him recently. We are just friends right now, Holly. I don't want to be in a relationship anytime soon. So, that kind of answers your second question as well.

I didn't believe her.

Right now? That says enough, Brooke. So, he hasn't been to your house twice this week?

How could I have been so stupid?

I don't know who told you that. Yes, he has been to my house, once to see my brother and another time to hang out and have tea. It was nothing more than that. I haven't kissed him, Holly. I haven't told him it's going to be anything more than what it is. How could you think I would just move on that quickly? Do you not remember the past four months? I'm insulted that you would think that of me.

I always remember someone telling me that people will admit to some of the truth to conceal the rest. I also remember someone telling me that a guilty person often becomes defensive and tries to turn the situation around. I didn't believe her, but I wanted to. If she had been able to move on that quickly, did she ever love me at all? Had I been nothing more than an experiment to her?

Men don't just 'hang out' with women unless they expect something more, Brooke, or they at least think it's going to be something more. So, that would tell me that you're giving him some sort of signals. I don't expect you to be honest with me, even though I think you owe me that. I thought I meant more to you than that, not just someone you could throw away after a few days. Did you ever have any intention of being with me? Did you ever really love me, or was I just an experiment to you? Something to pass the time?

My first glass of wine had already gone down at lightning speed. I took the bottle from the fridge and headed to the sofa once again. The reply from Brooke was waiting.

Well, I have made it very clear that is all I want, Holly. I don't expect you to believe me. Do you think you don't mean the world to me? You are all I think about 24/7. I have cried myself to sleep every single night this week. I sit at home and watch a movie or read a book, or I come across a picture of you, and all I do is cry because every damn thing reminds me of you. I love you with all my heart and I don't want anybody else, but one day, I will have to move on. We already knew that's how this would pan out, but that doesn't make right now any easier. You can sit there and blame me. You can try and make me out to be the bad person if that will make you feel better, but don't ever question my love for you because that is something that you cannot discredit.

All those conversations ever did was bring more harm than good. I wanted to go back to my dreams where everything made more sense; the world was round, the sky was blue, the grass was green, and me and Brooke lived a happy life together.

How wrong I was, thinking that confronting the situation would make it any better. Every time she told me she loved me, that I was the only one for her and that she would never love anyone the way she loved me, it was just another stake in my heart. There was a substantial list of all the things she had ever said to me, all the sweet nothings she had whispered, all the promises she had made and the love she had declared, but actions always spoke louder than words, and there were no such actions to match.

I can't do this anymore, Brooke. It's too hard to talk to you every day, to hear your voice, to reminisce with you the way we continue to do. I thought it would make it easier to move on, but the truth is, it's slowing the process down. One day, when you do move on (whether that be with Lewis or somebody else), it will break my heart all over again. I need to realise that this is over. The more you tell me you love me or you only want me, it makes it even more difficult for me to move forward.

My phone rang seconds after I pushed send.

"Hi, Brooke."

"Please just tell me you love me. I need to hear you tell me you love me and that you'll never forget about me. Please, Holly."

I could tell she had been crying.

"Why? You know that I love you. Why do you need the reassurance."

I didn't understand the need for confirmation.

"Because it could be the last time I hear it, and I need that. It's the last thing I'll ever ask of you, I promise."

Brooke continued to plead.

"I love you, Brooke Jacobs; that is the one thing I am certain of. I know that I will most likely always love you because a love like this only comes around once in a lifetime, and I will certainly…never forget you."

I tried to keep my composure and hold back the tears that were certain to come. It turned out that whether or not Brooke had entered into a relationship with Lewis didn't matter. What mattered was that we acknowledged everything that we were to one another and everything we would never be.

"Thank you, Holly. Just know that none of this was a lie. I wouldn't want that to be your last impression of me."

The energy to continue was there no more.

"Take care, Brooke. I'll always be here if you need me, but I think the best thing is for us to keep our communication to a minimum going forward."

I was fighting back the tears. It was time to move on and that was something I wasn't sure I was capable of doing.

"Okay, I understand. I'll always love you, Holly."

"Me too."

The next morning with a hangover that seemed incurable, I woke up to a knock at the door.

"Holly Garland, let me in please…wake up…wake up… come on, Holly."

It was Beth. I suddenly remembered that I was due to meet her at Nina's for one last breakfast before heading to the airport. The room was spinning, which made it more difficult to coordinate my body, but I managed to drag myself out of bed, hitting the door on the way out of the bedroom and banging my toe on the table in the hall. I eventually clambered my way to let her in.

"I am so sorry; I must have overslept."

Beth barged through to the kitchen and made herself at home. The kettle was already boiling before I even had time to shut the door behind her. The glimpse I caught of myself in the mirror as I made my way to the kitchen was one of a broken person. I excused myself for five minutes so I could freshen up.

Upon re-entering the kitchen, there was a fresh cup of coffee, some plain toast and two paracetamol accompanied by a big glass of water.

"You're the best, do you know that? Sorry again, I never usually sleep in this late."

Beth slid the paracetamol towards me as I sat down.

"I think we know the reason you slept in. Judging by the two empty bottles of wine and the bottle of tequila, your head must be feeling a little worse for wear this morning."

It didn't take a detective to figure that out.

"The wine was going down a little too easy. What time do you leave?"

"My flights at four this afternoon, so I can stay for an hour or so, then I'm gonna have to head to the airport. Do you want to talk about what you said to Brooke last night?"

Truth be told, I didn't want to talk about it; that was the last thing I wanted to do, but I knew I owed Beth some sort of an explanation for ignoring her the night before and then not turning up for breakfast.

"She denies it being anything more than friends, that she isn't ready for that and a lot of other stuff that isn't relevant anymore."

Beth's sceptical face said a thousand words.

"And do you believe her?"

I paused.

"I don't think it matters whether I do or not anymore, does it? It doesn't change anything. I guess time will tell."

"No, you're right, it will just hurt more for you if it is true, but maybe that's what you need to be able to move on from this. How did you leave the conversation?"

The toast was helping with the nausea; the conversation was not.

"I left it by basically saying goodbye. It's time to focus on myself. I have been holding onto what we had, so I didn't have to face the truth. It's over, Beth, there is no going back and it's time I realised that."

I could feel my eyes welling up; it was hard to stop the tears once they'd formed.

"Oh, H, I'm so sorry."

Beth stood up and walked towards me, offering her deepest condolences in the form of a well-needed hug.

"If I could change this for you, I would. It will be hard for a while, but it's nothing you can't overcome. Remember when Dale broke up with me and I was distraught? I wasn't sure how I would ever get over that, but here I am with a new and improved boyfriend, and I am the happiest I have ever been. Do you remember what you told me?"

I didn't remember. Dale was an inconsiderate, idiotic, sorry excuse of a man; that's what I remembered.

"I remember using an obscene amount of swear words, but that's about it."

She laughed.

"Yes, there was that, but you said something that has always stuck with me and now it's time for you to believe your own words. You told me my life wasn't defined by who broke my heart and that has stuck with me all these years because it's so true, Holly. We all think that we will never recover, but sometimes, two people just aren't meant for one another, and that's a fact of life."

'Your life isn't defined by who breaks your heart'. Words I hoped I could believe.

"Thank you for always knowing what to say. I'm extremely sad that you're going back to Tokyo. I will miss you so much."

We embraced for a few moments longer.

"I'm always just a phone call away; you know that. I'll always be here for you."

I would momentarily forget how much I loved having Beth around until she was home, and I remembered just how different life was without her.

She truly was my best friend and always would be.

CHAPTER SEVENTEEN

Six weeks later.

Time was a gift. You can't make more time, you can't buy it and you can't take it back. The most precious thing we have in life is time. How we choose to spend it and who we choose to spend it with is so important.

The time I chose to spend with Brooke, all be it was shorter than I would have wanted, was not a waste. It was a gift.

My contact with Brooke had been minimal after the final phone call. When we did speak, it was as freely as we ever had. I came to realise that there would always be a familiarity there; there would always be a sense of unfinished business and something that neither of us could deny; Love.

I had only seen Brooke once in those six weeks. She called at my house on the way to do some shopping so she could pick up a few of her belongings. The encounter itself was one of great difficulty. Just seeing her face, knowing I couldn't kiss her, was the most challenging part and that day briefly set me back.

We had spoken again about trying to be friends, but the thought was something I couldn't fathom so soon, although I hoped one day I could.

It was a Saturday morning, which meant I was home. My laptop was open and I was working on my current cases. A weekend off was very rarely an actual weekend off as I, more often than not, had 60 hours of work to fit into a 40 hour week, so there was always going to be an element of working from home.

The last time I had spoken to Brooke on the phone was almost two weeks prior, so when her name flashed up on my screen, I was surprised.

I contemplated letting it go to voicemail. I had a lot to do that weekend, and I didn't need something that might set me back, but given the circumstances, I thought it must have been something important, so I answered.

"Hi, Brooke, this is a surprise. Are you okay?"

She could probably sense that I was trying to hide the discomfort in my voice.

"Hi, Holly. I'm okay, thank you, are you?"

Enough of the chit chat already. What did she want?

"I'm doing okay. I assume you're not just calling me to ask if I'm okay, though?"

There was a slight delay.

"No, not exactly. I have some news, and I guess I wanted you to be the first person I told. Do you think you could meet me this morning?"

What news could she possibly want to tell me? I was instantly concerned.

"Some news? I'm assuming it's not good if you want to tell me in person. Can't you just tell me over the phone?"

Again, there was a delay at the other end of the line while my mind went into overdrive.

"Please, Holly, you'll understand why. I just want to see you and give you something."

So, she had something to give me? There was never any doubt in my mind that I would go and see her. The prospect actually excited me. Despite the heartache it brought, there was always the hope that maybe she would tell me something that I wanted to hear.

"Okay, when and where?"

She must have already been thinking about it because she answered without hesitation.

"Is 1 pm this afternoon okay? At Nina's? I haven't been since you took me a few months back; it would be nice to go again."

That worked for me.

"Sounds good. I'll see you there."

Nina's café was jam-packed, as it was every Saturday morning. The difference was that the ambience was more of a calm frenzy, not something that I had experienced through the week due to the overwhelming crowd of workers on a tight time scale.

My train had been right on time which was unheard of. This meant I had 15 minutes to kill until Brooke arrived. That wasn't too difficult to do, considering I was surrounded by coffee and breakfast.

My stomach felt squeamish from the moment I arrived. I tried my absolute best to overlook it, but that became more challenging the closer the clock got to striking one.

I must have checked my phone once every 30 seconds, mainly because it gave me something to do other than stare at the door. I wanted to see if Brooke had made any attempt to cancel. I thought of the prospect of her not coming at all, and that filled me with great sadness. As much as I knew seeing her would be difficult, not seeing her seemed a poor alternative.

Just when I was beginning to think she might not come, the door opened and she walked in. The ease in which she entered was enviable, unphased by the crowds of people and looking as beautiful as ever despite the turbulent weather outside. Her blonde hair was down and wavy but it looked slightly different. A hint of brown had been added. It suited her.

At first glance, the rest of her was exactly as it had always been. Her make-up was natural, just enough to make her skin glow but not too much that people would think she had tried too hard. She was wearing a pair of black jeans, Converse and a grey, knitted jumper accompanied by a camel coloured overcoat. Simple but elegant.

When she saw me, her grin was one of pure happiness. A grin I had missed profoundly but one that turned immediately back to normal. That disconcerted me.

Brooke approached the table and I wasn't sure what to do or the best way to approach the situation. I stood as she got closer and ushered her towards the empty seat to my right. I lingered for a second and then lent towards her to give her a brief hug. I felt her lips brush my cheek, and then her head fit softly into the side of my neck. The motion sent shivers down my spine, and it was as if the world stopped for a second; the only thing that mattered was Brooke's embrace.

The temptation to inhale the scent of Brooke's perfume was hard to refuse. She had always smelt so wonderful, a smell that I'd hoped would always seem so familiar to me.

When I pulled away from the embrace, our eyes locked immediately. I couldn't physically stop myself from smirking. The connection between us was indisputable, and the effect we had on each other was as apparent as it had ever been.

"You look good, Holly, really good."

Brooke assessed me from head to toe as she took a seat beside me.

"Thank you. You do too. Have you done something different with your hair?"

She inadvertently toyed with her hair upon me noticing it.

"Yes, is it really obvious? I just wanted a subtle tint of brown. I haven't done anything different with it in a long time, but I didn't want to change it completely. Do you like it?"

I loved it, just like I loved her.

"I do like it. It's subtle, but I'd like to think that me, of all people, would notice if your hair had changed."

Her smile was dejected. I swiftly remembered the reason she had wanted to see me.

"Brooke, what did you come here to tell me? I would rather just get straight to the point. I can see this is affecting you."

Brooke looked down at her phone, then at the coffee counter, then out of the window, then finally settled her gaze onto me. Since she called me that morning, all I had done was think of the possibilities. There was one logical reason why I thought she might want to speak to me in person. That involved Lewis. Where they now an item? Had she decided to take it to the next step with him like I had predicted all along? It seemed like the only possibility, what else could be so detrimental to me that she felt the need to tell me in person?

"Thursday morning, I found out that my dad's company is relocating him. Well, they have asked him to head up some business elsewhere, and they would make it worth his while. He hasn't given me and my brother much of a choice, to be honest. He thinks it will be good for the family to have a change of scenery and to experience a new culture."

Brooke was moving. What did that mean? Would she ever come back? Where was she going? A million questions ran through my mind.

"Wow, experience a new culture? Where exactly are you going?"

I could see tears begin to surface in her eyes. I reached out to hold her hand.

"Japan, Holly, he's moving us to Japan."

My whole body was in utter shock. Surely I must have been dreaming. The one person I loved more than anything in the world was about to move to Japan. How was that possible? The tears now streamed freely down Brooke's face.

"What? Are you serious? Why can't you stay here, Brooke? You're nearly 25 years old. Surely you can stay here? What about the house you live in now? I know your dad won't be selling it because of the memories, so why can't you just stay?"

I bombarded her with questions upon questions, and I couldn't stop to compose myself long enough to realise that none of it mattered. Brooke wouldn't be sat there telling me she was moving to Japan if she hadn't already made up her mind.

"Holly, please, it's more complicated than that and you know it is. What am I supposed to do? I promised my mum I would keep us together. I promised her I would look after him, Holly. I can't watch my dad go halfway around the world and not go with him."

There would always be that block between us. It infuriated me that she was so loyal to her father. He was willing to drag her across the world, away from her friends and everything she knew, because it was what he wanted to do. Everything was always on his terms, and she was so blinded by it.

"I have said this to you before, but seriously, when will you start living for yourself, Brooke?"

My tone was harsh, harsher than I had meant it to be.

"That's not fair, Holly. Please don't make this harder than it needs to be."

I moved my hand away from hers; maybe it was my way of coping with the situation. She was the only person I could focus my anger onto even though, deep down, I knew it wasn't her fault. Being so fiercely loyal and dedicated to your family weren't exactly the worst qualities one could have.

"So, why did you ask me here, Brooke? Surely you could have told me this over the phone?"

I quickly regretted my words.

"I'll tell you why Holly. The second my dad told me, I didn't think about missing my friends, where I would work, where we would live or even how I would learn Japanese, you know all the things you would expect someone to think about..."

She paused to wipe away the tears.

"...the only thing I thought about was you. How was I going to tell you? Not seeing you and trying to cut you from my life for the past few weeks has been the hardest thing I have ever had to do, but a part of me always felt like it was temporary. That, one day, we could maybe be friends or even more than that. I knew that you were only ever a phone call away, a 30-minute drive away, and I could see you if I needed to see you. The reality is that this move changes everything. It means that I truly have to let you go, and I truly have to continue my life without you in it. That is something I have tried to come to terms with for the past two days. That is why I asked you here."

My chest had tightened and the tears were now flowing. I tried to wipe them away whilst keeping some composure - after all, we were in a public place and I didn't want to cause a scene, but it was getting tougher by the minute to see Brooke so broken in front of me. Through all the many conversations we had and even the final break up conversation, I had never seen her reaction, never seen the heartbreak that engulfed her whole body.

Tears are an obvious sign of being upset - that is how we know someone is overtly sad - but I had never seen someone so physically and mentally broken. It was so much more than that; I knew it because her body reflected my own. She felt everything I had felt and more. I knew then that the love I had once doubted was so unbelievably real. Sometimes, it was as apparent as ever that love just wasn't enough.

I opened my mouth to respond, but she stopped me before I had the opportunity.

"I knew I would be a blubbering mess in front of you and that wasn't the last impression I wanted you to have of me, so I'm sorry. The reason I wanted to see you was to give you this."

Brooke reached into her bag and pulled out what looked like a letter. It was a white envelope that simply said *'Holly'* on the front.

She slid the letter over to me and proceeded.

"This is a letter from me. I have spent the last two days trying to put my feelings into words and then onto paper. All the greatest love stories I know involved letters. Noah wrote to Allie in *The Notebook*, Gerry wrote to Holly in *P.S. I Love You* and Savannah wrote to John in *Dear John*. So, I felt like I needed to write you a letter that you could look back on for the rest of your life, to know that what we had mattered. What we had was real and even if it wasn't our time, I didn't want you ever to forget just how much I loved you."

I picked up the letter from the table and turned it over, but Brooke stopped my hand before I had the chance to open it.

"Please wait until you're alone. Every word in that letter is true. Just promise me you'll keep it forever."

I instinctively reached toward Brooke's face to wipe the tears that were still falling.

"I promise I will keep it forever. I wish you would have told me. I didn't write you a letter."

Despite everything, she managed the tiniest smile.

"I didn't do it so that I would receive one in return. My memories of us will last a lifetime and I know that this has been especially hard for you, so I wanted you always to have this, to always know, even on your darkest days, that you were loved fiercely by me, and you always will be."

I kissed the back of her hand and smiled in return. The overwhelming feeling of sadness was one I didn't think I could bear. The brave face I tried to portray was precisely that, a brave face covering an overwhelming feeling of sorrow.

"Thank you for this. I will always love you, Brooke Jacobs, and I will miss you more than you could ever imagine."

"Ditto, Holly Garland. Always and forever."

There was nothing else to say other than a deeply regrettable goodbye to my soul mate.

I wasn't entirely sure how I ended up sat in my living room. The train journey home was a blur and my mind was so numb from the pain that I blocked out everything around me. The clock on the mantle said it was 4 pm. The life had been drained from my body and I had nothing else to do but open a bottle of wine and read the letter. I wasn't sure I was mentally prepared for the contents, but it felt like the final goodbye, one that, if anything, I hoped would soon bring me closure.

Dear Holly,

I have started this letter a thousand times and, every time I start to write about the beginning of you and me, I find it difficult. I will do this the only way I know how, from the heart.

I knew, from the moment I met you, that we would get along. I didn't think much about what we were or what we could be. I thought about how friendly and charming you were towards me and I wondered if you were like that with everyone.

It's hard to remember exactly how we became as close as we did. I know that I confided in you a lot; I spoke to you about anything and everything.

It wasn't until that first kiss in the underground that things changed for us. All of the conversations we had leading up to that night, all of the anticipation of what was to come, all lead us to where we are now.

Even now, all these months later, knowing what we know, I wouldn't change that night. I would not have done everything I did if I didn't love you as much as I do. If we are both honest with ourselves, I think we should have given up when we knew this wasn't going to be what we had planned, but the love I have for you would not let me. I physically could not let you go.

I don't think I have ever felt so many emotions at once, and the worst thing for me is that I don't get to hold you at night. I don't get to wake up to your beautiful face every day or have those lazy Sundays we both love so much. I can't walk through the streets holding your hand, and I can't kiss you in front of the world and be proud that you're mine.

I know that I will never love anyone the way I love you. I don't know what it is you do to me, but I barely even know how to function without you in my life anymore.

Whether you believe me or not, you really are the reason I wake up in the morning and, even now, when I see your name light up my phone, it still gives me butterflies like it's the first time. I need you to know just how madly in love with you I fell, how quickly you became my whole world and now, just knowing that you love me too, makes me the happiest girl in the world.

The truth is, I was scared to love you. I was afraid to let myself think of a future with you, but now I couldn't be happier that I did. I wouldn't have experienced half the things I did if I didn't let myself love you. You made me feel so special, so beautiful like I was the only girl you had ever laid eyes on.

Despite everything, Holly, I want you to be happy. I wish that more than anything, even though it breaks my heart to know that I am not the girl for you.

Promise me one thing, that you won't stand for anything less than perfect because you are perfect, and that is exactly what you deserve.

I never want you to forget me, and I hope that you always remember the way you feel now when you read this letter.

Every single day, I still try and prove my love for you. I know that I fail most days, but please know that, even when we argue or when we don't talk, or you feel as though I don't care anymore, I still love you more than life itself.

I love you more and more every single day, Holly, and I will never stop loving you. I want to say that I am deeply sorry I couldn't give you what you wanted; it will haunt me for the rest of my life. I still hold out hope that maybe, one day, things could be different.

Thank you for the happiness, sadness, excitement, love and everything you have given to me. You will never know how truly grateful I am to have had you in my life.

I am who I am today because you loved me.

You will have my heart, forever.

And I mean forever.

My love, always.
Brooke

In real life, love is very different from that in fairy tales.

When it comes down to it, love is just an emotion, and you need so much more to live.

The circumstances life throws at you don't allow you to live purely on emotion. Everyone has to be rational, think about consequences, cause and effect. As much as we all want to believe in fairy tales, sometimes, love just isn't enough.

I learnt that the hard way.

CHAPTER EIGHTEEN

The final goodbye.

Dear Brooke ,

Upon reading your letter, I felt the urge to write one in return. I wanted you to have something to look back on in the future. I guess I want you always to remember exactly what you meant to me and, more importantly, what you will always mean to me.

I can honestly say I have loved, but I have never loved anyone the way that I love you, and maybe I never will again.

From the first moment I kissed you, my mind was only focused on you. Distractions come and go; they always will, but what remains is you. We have been through so much in such a short period of time. So many ups and downs and enough tears to last us both a lifetime, but honestly, hand on heart, I wouldn't change a thing.

I love you now just as much as I ever have, and that will not change.

You will always be right for me, my perfect girl, the one I will never forget and the one I will always compare everyone else to.

Those first few weeks when I was getting to know you, I couldn't believe just how much we had in common, how alike we both were. Things were perfect in the beginning when we believed and hoped we could be everything we wanted. I know how difficult it was to put your own happiness second; it's something I have really tried to understand and often failed to. For that, I am sorry. Just know that I don't hold it against you.

I fell in love with you so quickly. We really did become each other's world, and even now, as I write this letter, I am crying as if I never stopped because the truth is I haven't. I never stopped being in love with you, I never stopped wanting you and do you know what the most heartbreaking thing of all is? We know what real love is. We know what it's like to love someone with every bone in our body, to want nothing but the very best for them, even when that isn't you.

You will always be such a big part of my life, even though you're moving halfway across the world and I don't know if or when I will ever see you again. There is one thing you will always have, a part of me that will always be with you, and that's my heart.

We were so happy at one point, and that's what I want you to remember. I would do absolutely anything for you, and I want you to know that, despite the time difference and the thousands of miles between us, I will always be here for you.

I don't know if it's just false hope, but I think about us one day finding our way back to each other. Maybe right now just wasn't our time; that's why we need to do the right thing and let go. If somehow we find our way back to each other, we know it was meant to be. If we don't, then I mean this next part with everything in me.

I want you to be happy, to live the life you've always wanted. I want you to find someone that loves you with everything they have and treats you perfect in every way because you deserve nothing less.

One day, in the future, you will be content with your life. Maybe you will be married; you might even have children. I hope you sit and smile when you think of me. I hope you take out this letter and remember us, remember the times we spent together and the memories we said we'd never forget.

Don't ever regret what happened or think about what might have been. What's done is done; it's all a part of life. We live, and we learn, but most importantly, we love. If there's one thing I can say, it's that I loved. I still love, I will always love.

In my eyes, you will always be my girl, my best friend, my soul mate and nobody will ever love you the way that I love you. I wish, every day, that I could've been the one to make you happy, and I still hope that I can, one day.

I still need you so much. I need you in my life and I will do everything I can to make sure you remain in it. I really do love you, and I will for the rest of my life. No one will ever take your place.

Don't forget about me, will you?

Always and forever yours.

Holly.

The final goodbye, the end of an era and the start of a new, unknown beginning, a place where many of us often find ourselves, hanging in the balance.

ABOUT THE AUTHOR

Nicole Spencer-Skillen is a number 1 best-selling author of Lesbian Romance and Fiction. Originally from Lancashire, England. She is 28 years old and happily married to her wife of 2 years. She has spent the last decade writing quotes, short stories and LGBT novels recreationally. When she is not writing, you will find her travelling the world, doing endless HIIT workouts or relaxing at home with her 2 dogs whilst dreaming up her next novel.

Lesbian romance is a genre Nicole is incredibly passionate about and she would love nothing more than to make an impact within this area. Growing up, she did not see herself represented in the books she read or in the book industry as a whole. Therefore, she predominantly read heterosexual romance novels, which happen to be some of her favourite books of all time, but they lacked the emotional pull she needed as she didn't feel she could fully resonate with the characters. That is why her aim is to write books that the LGBT+ community can connect with.

Nicole believes her writing to be real, honest and modern, but most importantly relatable. Her main aim is to appeal to the LGBT audience; the people who are looking for inspiration, especially the younger generation of gay women. She wants them to be able to see themselves in a book and resonate wholly with the characters.

Fun facts about Nicole, if she could live anywhere in the world it would be New York City. The city of dreams. Her favourite book is The Notebook by Nicholas Sparks of which she proudly owns a first edition. Her favourite sport is basketball, she proudly supports the Los Angeles Lakers and religiously watch's every game. She has a passion for quotes, after studying some of the most famous quotes throughout history. The one that resonates with her the most, is actually very simple.

"You miss 100% of the shots you don't take."

If you want to get to know her more, follow her on Instagram @nss_writings.

Lightning Source UK Ltd.
Milton Keynes UK
UKHW040814280421
382743UK00001B/81